A SUMMER TO CHERISH

BY

JOSIE RIVIERA

INTRODUCTION

To keep up on newly released ebooks, paperbacks, Large Print Paperbacks, audiobooks, as well as exclusive sales, sign up for Josie's Newsletter today.

As a thank you, I'll send you a Free PDF ... The Beauty Of ...

Josie's Newsletter

Did you know that according to a Yale University study, people who read books live longer?

5 STAR EDITORIAL REVIEWS

5 Star Crowned Heart InD'Tale Magazine Review and winner of the prestigious RONE award!

"When the main ingredient in David Fodero's artistic career threatened to shut everything that defines him, he withdraws from the rest of his world to a secret place where he hopes no one, from the life he is choosing to exit, can ever locate him. Ashley Madden who solely relies on David's art supplies, though indirectly, to keep her business alive, has to do something when the man holding the keys to her business disappears. Not knowing where to find him, she makes a trip to one of her close friends, Sarah, hoping to get a lead. True to her instincts, her friend gives her the much-needed help to locate the famous artist who has decided to shut the door to the business world. She barely knows the man. How will she even start questioning his disappearance?

What begins as a casual attempt to keep one's livelihood afloat takes a huge spin when the curtain of the artist's cool cabin split open. When the witty character of Ashley and the stoic no-nonsense stature of David mix, a rainbow of humor, hope, joy, and a great romance is born.

What an artistic piece of literary art!

The reader is totally carried away by the sequential waves of storyline that keeps the boat rocking, making it a perfect read for any day, any time. The theme of how to deal with people's disabilities through compassion shines throughout Ashley's role, making *A Summer to Cherish* a perfect mirror for the contemporary society.

Undoubtedly, lots of work, thoughts, and amazing talent went into what became this wonderful read. " - JM Lareen

AUTHOR ENDORSEMENT

"A delightful romance from Josie Riviera, reminding readers to value moments spent with those who fill our hearts with joy."

--SHANNA HATFIELD, USA Today bestselling author

5 STAR READER REVIEWS

"Sweet romance with a happily ever after. Obstacles can be overcome, and past troubles forgiven. Wonderful read."
   -Teresa, Amazon Reviewer

"It never ceases to amaze me when I read one of Josie Riviera's books. Her ability to create a beautiful sweet love story interspersed with deep abiding faith is truly a beautiful thing. A Summer to Cherish is a perfect example. Once again we are back in Cherish SC, a quaint southern town where it seems everyone shares the same faith and many of our beloved book friends are back. David Fodero, world-famous artist, has moved to Cherish to get away, and Ashley Madden, owner of an art studio for disabled children, has come in search of David. Their love story is so wonderful that you will want to keep reading far into the night until you get to their happily-ever-after. I know that I did!"
   -T. Echols, Amazon Reviewer

PRAISE AND AWARDS

USA TODAY bestselling author

#43 Amazon Contemporary Christian Romance Books

#75 Amazon Contemporary Christian Romance

CHAPTER 1

Every child is an artist. The problem is how to remain an artist once he grows up.
- Picasso

A famous artist didn't just disappear.

Ashley Madden steered her beat-up Chevy convertible around the final treacherous curve connecting her hometown of Greenwood, South Carolina, to Cherish, South Carolina. Earlier, a storm had kicked up, leaving a debris of tree branches and leaves. Fortunately, the trip took less than two hours to drive by car.

The route led her through the center of the town, which boasted peaceful, immaculate streets, brick-paved sidewalks, and a decided lack of skyscrapers.

She lowered her car window, drew in a breath of a rain-soaked breeze, and snagged the last peanut butter cup from her stash. She took a bite and exhaled a contented sigh.

Unhealthy food was definitely the tastiest.

Her gaze fixed on the road ahead, and she eased up on the gas pedal as she neared her destination. She kept her chin high, her eyes alert. This artist needed to be found, and she intended to find him. She was determined to preserve her free art program for handicapped children and their families low on funds.

Art made people think, made people feel. Art inspired her students to dance and jump up and down with joy.

And art lasted a long time—certainly longer than her relationship with her ex, who'd dumped her with a quick text:

Sorry it didn't work out between us.

And just like that, the relationship was over.

She eased her convertible into the first available parking space near Thumbs Up, a plant retail store and greenhouse. Squinting in the rearview mirror, she patted down her cowlick. Why couldn't it grow in the same direction as the rest of her hair?

It never occurred to her to fuss with her appearance. She didn't consider herself pretty—she was slight, though her feet were too big. People often remarked on her ready smile, though.

Today, she'd dressed in her typical uniform of a plain white T-shirt and chambray shorts. She couldn't imagine styling her honey-blond, shoulder-length hair other than tying it in a haphazard ponytail. Her makeup ritual consisted of sunscreen and a rosy lip gloss.

She shut off the ignition, unbuckled her seatbelt, then walked across the damp grass to the entrance of the greenhouse. Thick summer air hung heavy, the sun appearing through a gauze of humidity.

She shaded her eyes and peered at the sky. God's golden assurance, sunlight, was forever faithful. Regardless of the rain, He repeatedly guaranteed something better was around the corner.

Ashley entered the greenhouse, instantly recognizing the dark-haired woman engrossed in watering a pot of mauve African violets.

"Sarah?" Ashley came up behind her and tapped her on the shoulder.

Sarah whirled. "Ashley! Twinkle!"

Ashley smiled. Her nickname from a precious student. The name had stuck.

Sarah set the watering can to the side and tugged the apron from her slim waist. "How was the drive?"

"The roads are a mess from the windstorm." Ashley spoke slowly to help Sarah read her lips. Sarah had been diagnosed recently with a hearing loss and wore hearing aids.

"Were the roads littered with trees?"

"It could've been worse." Ashley embraced her friend in a hug. "However, I'm here and I'm fine."

"I'm due for my lunch break. Will you help me haul these bags to the storeroom first?" Sarah pointed to several bags of soil and sheepishly smiled.

Ashley returned the smile. "Of course."

Afterward, they headed toward the rear patio. Sarah grabbed a couple of bottles of water, a turkey sandwich on rye bread, chips, and a chocolate bar.

"Want to share?" She handed Ashley a bottle of water.

"Sure." Ashley slid onto a picnic table beneath a pink-flowered crepe myrtle tree. "I'll take the candy."

Sarah sat across from Ashley and whispered a prayer of grace before unwrapping the sandwich.

Ashley opened her candy bar. Chocolate, her favorite. "Any luck locating David Fodero?" she asked.

Sarah unwrapped her sandwich. "You mean, your reclusive painter?"

3

"He's not *my* painter. He's Nancy Trainor's painter," Ashley corrected between bites.

Sarah frowned. "Why would an artist like David have his work carried in a small gallery in a tiny southern town?"

"He and Nancy studied together in New York City. She decided her talent lay more in finding and promoting artists than in being an artist." Thoughtfully, Ashley chewed. "David is happy to help out her gallery by having her represent him."

Sarah raised an eyebrow. "Doesn't his artwork sell for tens of thousands of dollars?"

"He allows his works to be sold for lower prices in her gallery. The smaller pieces, not his large canvases." Ashley took another bite of her candy bar. "Without his paintings to sell, her gallery may close. The income his works provide allows her showroom to remain open. Luckily, he's prolific."

"Which implies your art studio will also be shuttered if he disappeared for a long haul," Sarah said.

"No one will rent me space as inexpensively as Nancy does. Plus, her showroom is a source of inspiration for my kids."

"So David Fodero isn't *your* painter, but the kids in your program are yours?"

Ashley grinned. "Every child is unique, and I love them all for their special talents and gifts."

She'd worked hard to make ends meet to provide for her students—whether it was brushes, soap, or an artist's table—and it was all worth it. Truly, she was blessed. She adored teaching kids and had shaped a satisfying career for herself.

"Maybe you can persuade David to donate funds for your art supplies." Sarah grabbed a chip. "He's certainly wealthy enough."

"If I can ever find him, I just might."

"Poor unsuspecting fellow." Sarah threw Ashley a smirk.

4

"He doesn't realize what he's in for. You don't put the brakes on until you achieve your goals."

"Poor unsuspecting, *mysterious* fellow," Ashley amended.

"It's odd no one has been able to reach him." Again, Sarah offered Ashley half her sandwich. At Ashley's refusal, Sarah happily finished it. "I wonder what happened."

"These genius artists are impossible. Nancy said he's very serious and oftentimes difficult. She walks on eggshells when she deals with him."

"I researched him on the internet." Sarah stood, indicating her break was over. "He is celebrated for his avant-garde portrayal of everyday subjects. Have you seen his *Woman by the River?*"

"That painting has been analyzed and torn apart by critics, though it's a fan favorite. When Nancy displayed it in her showroom, a student of mine, a nine-year-old girl with Down syndrome, continuously stared at it and smiled." Ashley's eyes welled. Her emotions, her affection for each precious child, brimmed inside her. "The girl didn't need any language to convey how she felt."

Sarah gave Ashley's hand a squeeze. "You care too much for people. You're eternally optimistic."

"I can't help it."

"That's why you're special. Don't ever change." Sarah retrieved the discarded wrappers and tossed them in the trash, along with their water bottles. Arm in arm, the women revisited the outside garden center before doubling back inside.

"For the record." Sarah's forehead furrowed. "I never figured out where the river actually was in David's painting."

"Neither did I."

"Who is the woman with the chestnut-brown hair in the corner?"

"Art enthusiasts have speculated about that for years. He's

been photographed with every leading actress on the planet. Perhaps the woman is one of them."

Ashley well remembered the day David Fodero had stridden into Nancy's showroom, the one and only time she ever saw him. He'd worn scruffy jeans and a casual navy-blue T-shirt. Yet he looked as handsome as when he'd been photographed wearing a black tuxedo at a glitzy fundraiser. His picture had been splashed on several society pages the following morning.

Nancy had confided he was growing tired of the endless social functions that demanded his attention, and he sought clean air and a calmer lifestyle in Cherish, a small Southern town not far from Greenwood.

Sarah gazed at the ceiling, as if David might miraculously appear. "He's drop-dead gorgeous, and every female on Earth wants to date him."

"Except you."

"I'm happily married to Max. But you're single."

"Yes." Ashley sighed. "Now and forever."

"Never say never." Sarah examined the African violet. Satisfied, she smiled. "Don't lose heart because of one failed relationship."

Don't lose heart.

What woman wouldn't lose heart after being dropped by a guy she'd dated on and off since college? Well-meaning acquaintances speculated she'd set the bar too high. Perhaps her ex couldn't live up to her expectations.

Which were what, exactly?

To show up when he promised her a date at the movies? To phone when he was out of town for long weekends?

Was there a man anywhere who was true to his word, a man who would sincerely care about her, and loved God as much as she did?

She shook off her reflections.

6

"I'm here on business to help Nancy." Ashley admired a particularly lush plant with cherry-red blossoms and considered buying it. However, she wasn't certain the plant would survive. Unlike her friend, her thumb was the opposite of green. "Nothing more."

"Unfortunate." Sarah sighed dramatically.

"Why?"

"You and David both like art. You couldn't ask for more."

"We're from two different orbits. He lives in New York City with a population of eight and a half million, while Greenwood has, what, five thousand residents?"

"Greenwood and Cherish are similar in size."

"A similarity we don't share with New York City." Ashley couldn't help a giggle. "It'll take more than art appreciation to ignite a spark between David and me. A distinguished painter and a woman who can't draw a stick figure to save her life isn't an ideal match."

"Perhaps." Sarah waggled her eyebrows.

Sarah, the incurable romantic. The women had shared a relaxed candor ever since they'd attended a friend's wedding five years earlier.

Bending, Sarah checked the water level of a particularly dry-looking violet. "David is better looking than your ex."

"Looks aren't everything."

"Looks are something."

"My ex is currently dating a knockout." Uttering the words aloud hurt, and Ashley pressed her lips together. "I saw them together at an upscale restaurant. Luckily, they didn't see me."

"You're a knockout too."

"Thank you." Ashley gnawed her bottom lip. Her ex had stripped away her self-confidence. In fact, he'd been cheating on her the entire time they'd dated. "However, I don't trust men anymore."

"All men?"

"Men in general."

"You enjoy reading romance novels."

"Those men are fictional."

"Never give up. Love will arrive when you least expect it." Sarah's tone was low and steady. "By the way, I discovered why David came to Cherish. Marge Addyson, the pastor of Memorial Street Church, commissioned him to paint a church portrait for their one-hundredth-anniversary celebration."

"And?"

"Last week, he was spotted on the church steps taking photos. Tall man with longish black hair, a trimmed beard, and crystal blue eyes, correct?"

"Yes. Or you could just say *brilliant and gorgeous*."

"Uh, huh. So I've heard."

Ashley belatedly pondered the wisdom of her description, although it was her first thought whenever she pictured him.

Sarah slid her a wise glance. "You know him better than any of the Cherish residents."

"I don't, because we never formally met. I only laid eyes on him for an instant when he appeared in Nancy's showroom to drop off a sketch. I was sitting on the floor of my adjacent studio, stenciling with an eleven-year-old boy. David glanced my way before he chatted with Nancy and gave me his legendary, wry smile."

"What did you do?"

"I smiled back, and we exchanged a friendly wave. His entire conversation with Nancy lasted all of five minutes before he dashed out the door."

She'd estimated he was several inches taller than her, which placed him at over six feet. Muscular and tanned, his physique contrasted sharply with her image of an artist—a thin, whiskered chap sporting a beret and wielding a paint-

8

brush. David's broad shoulders and masculine features were a stark reminder he was light-years beyond her—a teacher who spent her days amidst classes of giggling children, hanging art pieces on austere gray walls while complimenting drawings of princess castles.

Ashley shifted from foot to foot. "Nancy just sold his last oil painting and is adamant about connecting with him."

Much as she wanted to help her friend, Ashley's search for David Fodero was self-serving. Her studio and a café owned by a friend were both connected to Nancy's bustling gallery—a setup that benefitted all three businesses. If any failed, all would be left on rocky financial ground.

Ashley and Sarah reentered the store part of the nursery and were hit with a blast of cold air. The whir of an air conditioner ensured customer comfort from the relentless seasonal heat.

"People say he stays to himself and lives out on the edge of town." Sarah grabbed a metal watering can and filled it with water from a hose. "When my husband went bird-watching at Juniper Mountain yesterday, he saw David standing by his easel near a grove of trees."

"Where is Juniper Mountain?"

Sarah reached in her pocket and pulled out a discarded receipt. Flipping it over, she drew a makeshift map. "The mountain is in the state park. Max hikes the Walnut Forest route."

"Is it difficult?"

"Aren't you an exercise fanatic?"

"Sure. On a treadmill."

"Walnut Forest isn't challenging. David told Max he welcomes the solitude of nature and seemed absorbed in whatever he was painting."

"He is a true artist." Goosebumps rose on Ashley's arms whenever she envisioned his paintings. She speculated about

9

what inspired him to create his pieces—and why he chose certain textures and shades of colors, the scope of the canvases. "I wonder if he finished it."

His landscapes commanded thousands of dollars. It didn't matter what he painted. If patrons discovered his name signed on a canvas, they were willing to pay exorbitant sums.

"Trees, birds, and a pond were in the vicinity. I imagine those were in there somewhere." Sarah set down the watering can and began pruning a flamboyant-fuchsia flowering petunia. "Folks in town say he's polite, but his responses crackle the air like a broad band of heat lightning if someone dares to ask a personal question."

"He's known to be reclusive. Anything else?"

"I imagine Max led a painstaking description of all the birds in the park because he's the resident bird watcher." Sarah grinned. "But we all know how fiercely David guards his privacy, so few will infringe on that—not even talkative Max."

"Which may be why he hasn't answered any of Nancy's phone calls or texts for the past three months."

"He donated an oil landscape to Canine Helpers for their annual fundraiser—the cutest depiction of a dachshund who accompanies him everywhere." Sarah pulled dead leaves off the petunia. "At least, I think it's a dachshund in the painting. The dog's body is sketched in blue, and the ears are purple and red."

"Classic rebellious David." Ashley grinned. "Your information is appreciated."

"One more thing."

Ashley glanced at her watch. Sarah had been due to clock in ten minutes earlier. "I won't keep you any longer."

"No worries. I usually work overtime." Sarah brushed a piece of soil off her dark-green pants. "Max spoke with a park ranger who told him David purchased a dilapidated cabin a few miles outside the state grounds. He's been renovating it these past few months."

"That's where he's living? He bought a—Ashley made quote marks in the air—'dilapidated cabin'? He's not renting?"

"No. The cabin is on ten acres, bordered by state land on all three sides."

"What's the name of the road?"

"Pine Knoll Lane, and it's the only habitable property near the park." A wide smile crossed Sarah's face. "If you touch base with the ranger, he'll provide the general location. Although I warn you, solitude seems paramount to David."

"He's becoming a hermit."

"Right. So don't think you can just appear on his doorstep."

"I'm not here to marry him."

Sarah chuckled. "You're staying for the weekend, correct?"

"Yes. A substitute is teaching my Sunday school class." Ashley raked her hair from her forehead. "What time are the church services in town?"

"Memorial Street Church offers two services at 9:30 and 11:30. The pastors are outstanding, and the worship music is uplifting. I'll introduce you around if you attend."

"Count me in. I rented a room at the Cherish Hills Inn."

"Julian Wilson is the owner, and the church is a short walk from there. David drops by there for takeout meals, so maybe you'll meet him there."

"What are the odds? He may not stop in for another month." Ashley hesitated, then perked up. "Although a happy coincidence may occur."

Sarah frowned. "I've seen that look before. Are you up to something?"

"Have you ever heard the saying, if the mountain will not

11

come to Muhammad, then Muhammad will go to the mountain?"

"Sure. It means, if things don't go your way, then you change events so that they do."

Ashley tapped her fingers on a shelf stacked with clay pots. "Precisely."

"Are you Muhammad or the mountain?" Sarah tipped her head. "How can you run into someone who is rarely seen in public and doesn't answer his phone or email?"

"I'm whoever I need to be in order to locate him."

A foolproof plan had formulated. Well, perhaps the plan wasn't foolproof, but it was a start.

Her instincts shouted *no*. The plan was filled with the likelihood of failure, although she couldn't think of anything better.

She dismissed her reservations because her brain shouted yes.

Ashley was Muhammed. And Muhammed was going to the mountain.

CHAPTER 2

Art is a lie that makes us realize truth.
- Picasso

*D*avid had spent the entire day painting. Or, more accurately, attempting to paint.

He stood at his easel surrounded by oak trees, a jewel-like river bubbling in the distance. Shadows cast by the branches shielded him and his dog from the sun. He'd brought water for them both, in a thermos and doggie dish respectively, as well as an energy drink for himself.

New Yorkers who were accustomed to snow and temperatures below freezing weren't supposed to be fond of penetrating summer heat. Yet he relished everything about Cherish, including the weather. This quintessential Southern town was proving private and off-the-grid, boasting natural beauty and a sunny climate. In just a few months, he'd met more sincere, down-to-earth folks here than in his entire two decades in a large, impersonal city.

As the afternoon gave way to early evening, the sun glowed with a burning hue.

The golden hour. The hour most flattering. The light was diffused, the silhouettes intense.

"Red and soft and magical. Right Pickle?"

His dog looked up at him with shiny oval eyes and angled his head.

David grinned at his devoted dachshund, consistently in tune with him and his moods. Pickle's long, low body always seemed balanced, his black-and-copper coat smooth, his demeanor curious. Never farther than a few trots from his master, Pickle proved that adopting a dog from a pet rescue center was one of David's finest decisions.

He stood back from the easel to assess his work.

One tree.

Two endless weeks of sweat, countless energy drinks, and one tree.

What was he doing? Anyone could paint a tree. A child could paint a tree.

Just because he'd framed the tree in a garish-orange stained glass window didn't make it any better. Any more unique. There was a fine line between avant-garde and absolute nonsense.

He tossed down the last of his energy drink and regarded the river, the sun's rays glittering along the water's surface. Some days, the anger and sadness at his loss subsided, as he appreciated the splendor of his surroundings.

Not today.

His designs from earlier years had been described as radical and unorthodox, and he'd been acclaimed as a prodigy. Newer pieces were applauded because of his experimental approach to design and color.

When he'd first become recognized, he'd scoured every email and text he received, checked the tweets that mentioned him, holding out hope his older brothers would recognize his contribution to the art world. If they did, they hadn't bothered to inform him. And his father? Hardly a word of praise, even when David used to phone him on weekends. Their relationship had always been strained.

Once, he'd fantasized about moving back to the mid-sized city where he was born and purchasing the original homestead, just to prove he could. He'd amassed enough money with his art sales to buy the entire city. His livelihood was effectively guaranteed and predicted to become even more impressive.

But currently?

Though too soon to determine, he was certain he'd despise his latest piece when it was finished. Inspiring paintings didn't come easily anymore. In retrospect, they never had.

Neither did innovation. All artistry required direction, analysis, and exceptional ideas to execute, with a healthy dose of diligence and confidence.

He wanted to create pieces the artistic community had never seen before. He wanted to rescue his career. The sad truth was he hadn't liked anything he'd painted the past few months. Not since he'd woken up one morning, barely able to see out of his right eye.

He was an artist. This wasn't supposed to happen to an artist.

So what?

He had nothing left to prove. He'd accomplished every artistic milestone at a relatively young age.

The knowledge he could no longer paint anything worthwhile left him humbled and dispirited. He'd considered other art forms—perhaps picking up his oboe again or writing poetry—for fulfillment. Or purchasing another estate, or docking a yacht on an exclusive island, or escorting a starlet to a dazzling social gathering.

He couldn't bring himself to engage in any of those activities anymore. A part of him—ethics, morality, the boy who had once believed in God—was dejected by a shallow, affluent lifestyle.

So much for doctors. So much for irony. So much for God ... taking away an artist's eyesight. What sense did that make?

"C'mon, Pickle." David grabbed his easel and paints, and then picked up his ten-pound dog, being sure to retrieve the dog's favorite toy—a plush, striped elephant.

David buckled Pickle into the dog car harness in the back seat of his crew-cab pickup truck. Then he buckled himself in the front seat and drove the short distance to his cabin. He had no trouble driving. Just as his ophthalmologist had predicted, David's brain had adjusted to compensate for the loss of depth perception.

"You'll be fine," the doctor had assured him.

Right. What, exactly, described *fine*?

Claude Monet, the French Impressionist painter, suffered from cataracts, and his eyesight had been impaired as he aged. He'd complained of foggy vision and undergone surgery. His paintings had changed as a result of the deterioration.

David certainly shouldn't compare himself to Monet, but he recognized his work was shifting—and not for the better.

He pulled his truck into the gravel driveway of his home and regarded the remote area and vast acreage. His cabin was concealed from the road by thick woods.

Rustic, yet remarkably well-appointed following David's renovations, the cabin offered an ideal retreat. The timbered ceiling was braced by beams of weathered cedar, and a spiral staircase led to a bedroom loft, which offered a panoramic view of forest and mountains. On a vibrant, sunny day, the scene was magnificent.

He kicked off his shoes as soon as he entered. The hours ahead promised peaceful solitude and reflection. In winter, a crackling fire in the massive stone fireplace would be a requirement. For a June evening in the Carolinas, he'd opt for a riveting adventure thriller audiobook, while he and his dog settled in his favorite chair, a redwood armchair. He prized the exposed rustic tree knots and polished design.

In former years, devotions to God would have highlighted his reflections, as well as Bible study. He especially enjoyed reading from the Old Testament. When despondent, he had absorbed the poetic, inspiring psalms that described God's love and mercy. The words had entered him like an inspirational melody.

Those were days long past.

God had taken too much away. As a result, he maintained a distant relationship with God. His plea for help had never been answered.

David's foundation was gone, his faith unfocused.

The feeble protest of his conscience to utter a prayer, any prayer, fell by the wayside.

With a harsh sigh, he gazed out the living room's front bay window. Flecks of dust danced in the pitch of afternoon sunlight. The windowpanes needed dusting.

Aware of the fleeting minutes, David regarded the plot of land he considered ideal for a garden. He'd never tended soil. Perhaps now he would. A garden offered order to the forest, direction for his thoughts.

He scratched his temple. What vegetables and flowers grew under a fierce summer sun? Was June too late in the season for planting?

His deliberations drifted to work and obligations.

Tomorrow, he'd begin sketching the commissioned

painting of Memorial Street Church he'd agreed to finish by summer's end. He'd taken various photographs of the church's white painted exterior, ornate wooden doors and high-arched windows, from different angles.

He threw an ironic glance at his reflection. How could he complete a project he hadn't begun? Procrastination wasn't his style, though with a few words, the ophthalmologist's diagnosis had altered everything.

David's optic nerve to his right eye wasn't getting enough blood. He was slowly going blind.

AN HOUR LATER, after a quick shower and dressed in his usual T-shirt and jeans, he situated himself on a bench facing the tree painting. He couldn't help himself, couldn't stay away from painting. Pickle sat on a woven wool rug, his striped elephant beside him.

A tap on the door brought David and Pickle to their feet.

No one visited. No one, thankfully, knew exactly where he lived.

With an irritated shake of his head and the dog at his heels, he padded to the entry.

A slight, dainty woman stood on the porch steps, dark glasses covered her eyes, her blond hair swinging from a side part and spilling to her shoulders. Wayward, shiny strands drifted across her cheek. Dappled sunlight shone through towering pine trees, and shadows formed on the ground. Somewhere, the fluttering of unseen wings broke the silence.

Her figure was slender. The thought came to mind that a strong windstorm could blow her off her feet.

"Hi." Her voice was bright and breezy, resembling her appearance.

"May I help you?" He opened the door wider. "If you're selling cookies, I'm not buying."

18

"Who said I was selling cookies?"

"You don't look any older than a university student."

"Do university students sell cookies?"

"For fundraisers, I suppose."

She paused. "Do you have any?"

"University students?" He glanced over his shoulder. "Nope."

"Funny. Not."

"Oh, you're referring to cookies." He surveyed her from the top of her smooth forehead down to her manicured toes, peeking out from strappy sandals. She wore slim-fitting jeans and a green floral blouse. Her complexion was healthy, a sun-kissed tan along her cheeks and the bridge of her freckled nose.

He grinned. "I stored a couple boxes of cookies in my freezer."

"What kind?"

"Chocolate with a creamy-white filling."

Her generous lips pulled into a smile. "My favorite. I have it on reliable authority most cookies thaw quickly, though I've often eaten them frozen."

He patted his stomach. "I've inhaled half a box in one sitting."

"Frozen?"

"Microwaved."

Inwardly, he shook his head. They were actually discussing cookies. If this was considered lighthearted conversation, it felt foreign. He had forgotten the pleasure of conversing with a lovely, quick-witted woman.

She slid the dark glasses down her nose. Huge, hazel-green eyes flicked him a glance.

A shadow of a smile crossed her lips. He wasn't sure why.

With an about-face, she gestured toward a blue Chevy

convertible parked in front of his cabin. "Unfortunately, I'm stranded."

"I'm sorry. Trouble with your car, ma'am?"

"Miss." She plucked off her glasses and perched them on her head.

They locked gazes.

Time stood still.

He wasn't an overly emotional guy, yet feelings that hardly made sense bombarded him. Attraction, an instant connection, a familiarity he couldn't explain.

"My convertible stalled, and my cell phone battery is dead." Her statement sounded far away, and he dragged his mind to attention.

"I'd offer assistance." He scanned the road. "Regrettably, my skills as a mechanic are sorely lacking." *They were, in fact, nonexistent.*

"May I use your phone to call a friend? I don't intend to drive these deserted roads at night. The curves are difficult to navigate."

He peered outside. The sky was etched in pinks and grays. Dusk set slowly in the Carolinas, and darkness wouldn't occur for another hour. "You're on Pine Knoll Lane. I'm surprised you made it this far without realizing there's no outlet. Loop around, and you'll connect with the state park entrance in a few miles."

"Once my car is running again." Her tone was easygoing, her smile angelic. "My sense of direction is faultless, though I obviously lost my way."

"Obviously." He shifted. Why was he thinking this woman was special? He didn't even know her. "If you're looking for a tree-lined residential street, head to Cherish. There's nothing of interest on this road."

"There are lots of things of interest." She caught his stare, then turned to peer at the deserted road. "I planned to hike Grandfather Mountain today."

"Isn't Grandfather Mountain in North Carolina?"

"Oh."

Oh? She was in the wrong state?

"I'm a mountain climber."

She certainly didn't look like a mountain climber, and she didn't know her mountains very well, either. Where was her backpack, and why wasn't she wearing sturdy shoes caked with mud? Her sandals were white and clean.

No business of his. Perhaps her gear was packed in her car.

Still, why hike at dusk?

He watched her in silence. Soon she'd be on her way. The sensations that raced through him, that instant flare of attraction, would soon disappear.

"May I use your phone?" she repeated.

"Certainly. C'mon inside. I left my phone in the kitchen."

"Thanks." She offered a helpless laugh. "I hope I'm not putting you out."

He glanced at his canvas by the window and reminded himself that people were more important than work. He strove to achieve balance, although it wasn't easy.

"You're not putting me out at all." He led her into the living room. The worn hardwood floors creaked beneath their feet, and he motioned to the L-shaped sofa. He suspected the sofa hailed from the 1960s, judging from the plaid pattern and velvet armrests, but it was clean and homey and comfortable. He hadn't replaced all the furniture yet. Likewise, he hadn't gotten around to a kitchen remodel.

Pickle trotted beside them and sniffed the woman's sandals. Quickly surmising she was a friend, he brought his striped elephant close to her and flopped on his back for a belly rub. She accommodated him while cooing that he was

21

the cutest dog in the county. Judging from the dog's rapturous pose, her compliment delighted him.

"Adorable." She nodded at the elephant.

"His favorite toy."

"I've never owned a dog."

David looked at her as if she'd uttered a statement entirely foreign to him.

"I can't," she explained. "I've fantasized forever about adopting one, but my apartment is tiny, and I spend most of my days and evenings at my studio teaching." She smiled. "I love animals, though."

"Visit your local rescue center, adopt a miniature chihuahua, and bring the dog with you to your studio."

"Helpful advice." Her smile faltered. "Perhaps someday."

"Someday." David glanced from her to Pickle.

"You can't beat a pet to combat loneliness." She went on rubbing Pickle's stomach. "Animals help humans reconnect with nature. Some say dogs are God's messengers because they grant us grace."

"Pickle is a significant part of my life. He's my comrade."

She looked up at him, her gaze sparkling. "Pets are extraordinary."

He nodded in agreement and headed for the kitchen. "Extraordinary, indeed."

He reached in the freezer for a box of cookies and decided on bottled water instead.

Retracing his steps into the living room, he asked, "You're not from around here?"

"No."

He had assumed she'd be sitting on the sofa, rubbing Pickle's belly.

She wasn't.

Pickle was snuggled in his doggie bed by the fireplace. She stood facing David's unfinished tree painting.

She refused his offer of hospitality by shaking her head at the water and gestured to the painting. There hadn't been graffiti on the tree, although he'd added it, enhancing the graffiti in bold purple letters. The blue sky, devoid of clouds, conveyed a curious juxtaposition against the solemn moss-green grass. Carroty stained-glass windows stood out sharply in the background.

She surveyed the canvas. "Is this a happy or sad painting?"

He set the water bottles on the coffee table, noting she hadn't answered his earlier question about where she was from.

"Paintings don't have feelings."

"People do."

He clasped his hands. "I haven't decided."

"About people's feelings or the painting?"

He didn't reply. Instead, he handed her the phone and provided her with the local mechanic's number.

"Thanks." She focused on the canvas. "All your paintings bring up complicated emotions."

"All? How do you—?" She must be an art enthusiast who recognized his work. He was obliged for the support, though lately he couldn't muster any sentiments—gratefulness, productiveness, motivation. Everything he'd taken for granted had evaporated when he'd received his eyesight diagnosis.

She wandered away with his phone to her ear, muttered a few sentences, then disconnected. "I called my friend who can repair anything that goes wrong with a car."

Already feeling useless as an artist as well as a mechanic, David murmured, "Good." If he were one of his brothers, he would've dashed to her car, yanked the appropriate tools from his pickup, and fixed the problem for her.

He wasn't that kind of man, though. He'd never been mechanical.

Left brain, right brain, he theorized. He was the opposite of a methodical thinker. His right-brain dominance made him creative, prone to day-dreaming, intuition, and visualization.

"No tools here beyond a couple screwdrivers and a hammer." He shrugged. "My truck is loaded with canvases, watercolors, and an easel."

"No worries. Everyone can't be a pro at everything."

"Your worldview theory?"

"I look at life through God's perspective."

Noncommittally, he shook his head. "Whatever works for you."

She peered at him. "You sound like you're hard on yourself. Are you?"

"Not enough to be psychoanalyzed in my own living room."

"Right." She chewed her lower lip. "So, my friend will be here soon."

The longer he gazed at her, the more familiarity niggled, though he couldn't place her. Her blond hair was a hundred shades of gold. Those startling hazel eyes seemed to change from green to brown at will. Doe-eyed. Perceptive and luminous.

He cleared his throat. These intense feelings roused recollections of his teenage years over two decades earlier.

He bent to go after a paintbrush lodged under the sofa. "How long?"

"Hmm?" She stepped closer to his canvas.

"How long?" he repeated.

"How long what?"

He stood. "How long before your friend arrives?"

"Not long." She laser-focused on the painting. "This tree really is magnificent."

"You figured out it was a tree?"

24

"Yes. Is that good news or bad news?"

"For an avant-garde artist, I'd consider it bad news."

She folded her hands behind her back, peering at the landscape. A clear invasion of his privacy. Then she fixated on the rusted coffee can on the fireplace mantel.

"Quite an unusual decoration," she noted.

"Thanks." He searched for an explanation and decided on none.

"And the redwood chair in the corner is … rustic."

"I moved it here from my Manhattan apartment." He set the paintbrush in a bucket. "I helped create the design."

"Is it comfortable to sit on with all that wood jutting out all over the place?"

He smiled. "Chair pads soften the experience."

"The sitting experience."

He chuckled. "Correct." He couldn't stop drinking in the sight of her slim figure. Her jeans hugged her curves to perfection.

What? He gave himself a mental shake. He was seeking a laid-back lifestyle without complications. Perhaps then he'd be inspired to paint something worthwhile.

She concentrated on the coffee can. "Is there an artistic significance in that?"

"Maybe." He crossed his arms, narrowed his gaze.

"Is the living room your studio?"

"This room gets the most favorable light in the house since it faces north."

Canvases slanted against the walls, wrong side out. She gestured to them. "Do you ever show your work?"

"No." True enough since he'd moved to Cherish.

"Why not? You should paint often and sell everything."

To dissuade her from asking any more questions, he flashed her a frown. "Look miss, I don't even know your name."

Not losing a beat, she held out her hand. "Ashley Madden."

He tilted his head to the side. In some way, the name was recognizable too.

He took her hand and shook. Her fingers were fragile and delicate, sending a warm tingle through him.

Indeed? For a woman's hand? He really needed to get out more.

"David Fodero," he replied.

Admiration shone in her gaze. "Hello, David."

"Likewise, Ashley."

She arched her graceful blond eyebrows. "*Likewise?* Quite the introduction."

"I'm not known for flowery words. What I meant was ..." His formal upbringing kicked into gear. "My pleasure."

He assumed he'd let go of her hand, but peering down, he realized he hadn't.

"My friend should be here within a half hour." Ashley continued their earlier conversation as if no lapse had occurred, then dropped her hand. "I assume that's okay?"

Did he have a choice? "Of course."

"Why not?"

He took a sip of water. "I'm not following." Clearly, this woman shifted topics with the speed of a tornado.

"Why not show your pieces? Your art is thought provoking."

Respect threaded her tone. He recognized it, appreciated it, but couldn't respond except for a nonchalant, "My work isn't good enough."

"You're joking, right? Surely you don't believe such a thing."

"It's my opinion, which is the only opinion that matters."

He indicated they should sit, and they chose either ends of the sofa. She was silent. He was well aware she had set

26

aside her curiosity and inquiries about his paintings because of his blunt reply.

"I have iced tea in the fridge." His statement broke through the silence. "Care for a glass?"

"No, thank you." She shot him a measured smile across the breadth of the sofa. "I prefer sugary soda."

"I'm an energy-drink guy."

"I noticed." She darted a glance at the empty cans in the wastebasket near his bench.

His brain faltered for something else to say. He wasn't chatty—unless discussing art or photography—and lately even those subjects made him uncomfortable.

He gazed around the room for a way to restore their earlier banter because he regretted the loss. Playfully and without thinking, he tossed a fringed throw pillow at her.

She let out a startled shriek. The dog leaped up, barked, and circled the table. The friendly mood returned as Ashley laughed and threw the pillow back at him.

"Don't you dare!" She held up a hand to fend off another throw.

"Give up?" He stood and swung the pillow back and forth. "What's a little pillow fight to a seasoned mountain climber?"

"You're right. You win." She switched an innocent smile on him before grabbing another pillow from the sofa.

A knock brought their hands to their sides. Ashley tidied the pillows they'd disarranged. With her pink cheeks and a sparkle in her eyes, she created a fetching picture.

"Now who might that be?" He rubbed his chin. "Someone else selling cookies?"

She grinned, peeked out the window, and waved. "I'll get it."

"Be my guest," he mumbled with wry courtesy.

Her laughter rang out as she opened the door. An auburn-haired woman stepped inside.

"David Fodero, meet Sarah Archer," Ashley said. "She's my handy repair person."

A woman.

Sarah offered a hello and took a step back. Reserved and a bit shy, he mused.

"All set, Twinkle," she said to Ashley.

Twinkle? David opened his mouth to inquire about the name, but Ashley ignored him.

Sarah mumbled something about a mysterious engine part, and Ashley responded by using sign language.

Wait. Ashley's friend was deaf?

Sarah offered him an abashed smile. "I'm losing my hearing. I denied it for ages, until my husband, Max, prodded me to confront my fears and visit an audiologist. I believe you met him at the state park."

"The birdwatcher who always wears a bow tie?"

"Yes." Sarah smiled. "Now that I've adjusted, my hearing aid is a blessing, along with signing."

He turned to Ashley. "You know sign language?"

"I run an art studio that's attached to a couple other businesses, one being a café." Ashley reached for her water bottle. "A waitress who works there is deaf."

"You own a business?"

"Yes, for handicapped students. I cared for my dad when I was young and missed a lot of school. I fell behind and the teachers labeled me as a slow learner. After a while, I quit trying. Then I met a wonderful mentor, and he was an inspiration. From then on, I vowed to help others." She waved a dismissive hand. "More information about me than you would ever possibly want."

"No, not at all." He was still reeling from this personal insight about her. "Is your studio in Cherish?"

"No."

More questions came to mind.

Before he could inquire, Ashley gestured to Sarah. "My friend has the greenest thumb on the planet."

He considered congratulating Ashley for another rapid subject change. Instead, he remarked to Sarah, "I've contemplated planting a garden."

"I work at Thumbs Up, the nursery in town." She pulled a business card from the back pocket of her jeans and handed it to him. "Give me a call."

"Thanks." He pocketed the card and glimpsed the two women, a little unnerved at the smile that passed between them.

Sarah eyed his dog, who had permanently attached himself to Ashley. Crouching, she rubbed his stomach. It was amazing what dogs did for a belly rub.

Sarah glanced up at him. "What type of plants are you interested in?"

"Whatever will grow in this hot sun."

"I recommend zucchini and squash and carrots."

"Sugar-coated carrots are delicious," Ashley chimed in.

"All my favorites," he joked, then sobered. "I'm sorry. I'm not sure how to converse with you, Sarah. I never studied sign language."

She stood. "I read lips and understand you perfectly."

"Are you a musician?" He perched his hip on the edge of the redwood chair.

Both women frowned in confusion, and he immediately regretted his words. But Sarah's disability had made him think of his own—although it was constantly on his mind anyway—and he'd wondered if she was an artist too.

"My husband plays harmonica and is in a band with my uncle," Sarah answered. "Why?"

Were they really discussing musicians? Yes, and he had initiated it.

29

He peeked at Ashley. This woman knew hardly anything about him, yet he sensed her interest in his answer.

His muscles tightened. He was up for the challenge.

"Beethoven suffered from deafness." He picked up his water bottle and rolled it between his hands. "Any theories why that would've happened to him?"

Ashley regarded him with a sideways glance. "I'm not certain."

"I assume you'll lay it on God. That He works in mysterious ways."

"Often, He does." She stood straighter. "Faith is fragile. Faith takes time. Hold on to faith when there's too much of life and too little of you."

"Is that what Beethoven did?"

"I don't know."

He sighed heavily. "Therefore, according to you, I should take a step toward believing in God."

"God is always working on a solution."

How had this become a theological discussion?

"Then tell me this," he challenged. "Is a musician losing his hearing comparable to a painter losing his eyesight?"

He saw the shock in Ashley's eyes, knew when the impact of his words struck her.

She pressed a hand to her lips. "David, is there anything—?"

In the soundless aftershocks, he kept his features bland and didn't answer. He'd revealed too much already and hoped she wouldn't read into his response.

"DAVID FODERO IS GOING BLIND?" Ashley whispered to Sarah as soon as they left David's cabin. The women stepped along a stone path and hastened to their cars. Rather than broaching the subject further, Ashley had opted to remain

30

silent. Sarah had wordlessly agreed. Besides, he'd quickly banished any questions by his cool response. Or rather, lack of response.

"He wasn't necessarily referring to himself," Sarah said.

"Of course he was." Ashley tried not to appear as troubled as she felt. The pride stamped on his face, the jut of his chin, declared that David Fodero wasn't the type of man who resigned himself to his fate. Yet there was a profound sadness in his eyes. "Who else might he be referring to? Van Gogh?"

"I thought Van Gogh was supposed to be color blind."

"Judging from David's voice, he was referring to his own disability. I want to help him find a solution."

"Your infinite optimism is surfacing again." Sarah inclined her head toward the cabin, then at Ashley. "You constantly try to solve other people's problems. Rest and leave it to God."

The air was eerily stagnant, the sun beginning its descent as Ashley and Sarah hugged each other goodbye. As soon as she reached her car, Ashley leaned her head against the door to collect herself. Her chest knotted at the awareness of David's blindness. Despite his attempts to sound casual, his expression and deep voice had revealed raw emotion.

Now she knew the reason why he hadn't responded to Nancy's emails, phone calls or texts. Ashley's heart missed a beat at the image of his troubled, handsome face. The consequences of his disability plagued her long after she'd retired to Cherish Hills Inn for the evening.

She sat on the cozy white comforter on her bed, drew up her legs, and wrapped her arms around her knees.

He wasn't blind *now*. He'd looked at Ashley as if he saw her with no trouble. He didn't seem to encounter any difficulty moving from room to room. And he obviously still painted.

His depiction of the tree was wonderful. Different from

31

his earlier works, this canvas was darker, more melancholy. According to well-informed art critics, David's talent was phenomenal, an unstoppable force that had shaken up the art world.

She couldn't make that sort of judgment. She simply respected his talent and skill, his distinctive portrayals of nature and everyday life expressed his recognizable style.

In Greenwood, she was on a mission to make a difference, providing an art platform for handicapped children.

In David's case, surely his condition could be treated by a skilled physician.

And prayer.

CHAPTER 3

Art washes away from the soul the dust of everyday life.
- Picasso

Sunday, Ashley rose early and breakfasted in the inn's solarium. The room had been recently added onto the original building, a hostess explained. Benefitting from the natural light, the lavender paint on the window trim and the pops of greenery, along with white wicker tables and chairs, completed the cheery environment.

The breakfast offerings included fluffy French toast drenched in pure maple syrup and black coffee that Ashley doused with sugar and cream. All served by Samantha, a pleasant young waitress with ice-blue eyes and dark hair. She worked during her summer break from college, she explained to Ashley. Her father was the owner.

"No work-out room?" Ashley asked, scanning a colorful pamphlet with descriptions of the inn's services.

"Sure, we do." Samantha gestured toward the hallway. "Complete with a weight machine and treadmills."

Ashley made a mental note to exercise the following day.

As she watched the comings and goings of other diners, she focused on how next to approach David.

The prior evening had gone as planned. She'd found him at his cabin.

Her breath had caught at how good-looking he was—wearing jeans and a white T-shirt that clung to his wide shoulders. His hair was rumpled, his strong jawline appealingly stubbled. He'd padded barefoot through the living room, his strides long and purposeful, and he'd been welcoming, inviting her to make herself comfortable.

She'd felt a strong attraction to him, a pull she couldn't deny.

With a nervous lungful of air, she'd seized the chance to study his one visible painting when he went into the kitchen for his phone. Of course, she hadn't needed to phone Sarah, and a tinge of remorse for her deception tightened her stomach.

Soon, she'd reveal to David the real reason she'd come to Cherish. She'd also acknowledge she was mechanically inclined and could've fixed her own car if something had actually gone wrong.

She attributed her self-reliance to her father. He'd raised her as a single parent and made certain she could take care of herself. He had also been a devoutly religious man, frequently reminding her that God knew her life from beginning to end—and to release any burdens she carried to God.

She'd vowed to pass her father's teachings along and did what she could to minister to other people.

A peaceful determination swept through her, banishing any reservations and leaving her mind sharper. She was here for a reason.

Yes, to help Nancy. But something more.

God's hand was imperceptible, but He was never idle.

That flutter of excitement? The butterflies in her stomach when she and David had locked gazes? She dismissed it as a passing attraction.

Nevertheless, her reaction confused her. She couldn't get him out of her mind.

She drained her coffee and left the restaurant with a fast-paced stride, phoning her two part-time employees and asking them to cover her for the upcoming week.

She stopped at the lobby and extended her stay, then walked the few blocks to Memorial Street Church. Sunday mornings were meant for more than a leisurely breakfast and steaming coffee. Sunday mornings were meant for reverence and allowing God to provide a path. Specific details? They weren't needed. All that was needed was trust.

AFTER BEING SEATED for dinner at the inn's restaurant later that evening, Ashley spotted a painting on the wall. The landscape—wildflowers, trees and water—seemed to be in David Fodero's familiar signature style. The colorful wild-flowers were upside down, the bubbling river noticeable only if an observer looked closely. David's brushwork was detailed, his design abstract.

She was so lost in thoughts of him, it took a few seconds for her to realize the owner had approached her table.

"Complex, isn't it?" Julian Wilson, a tall man with gray eyes, held a silver water pitcher. He eyed David's painting as he filled her glass.

"Thanks." Mesmerized, she perched her chin on her hands to continue to stare at the painting, then turned to him.

She'd spoken with Julian on several occasions when she'd

made her reservation. He was always pleasant and helpful and seemed able to accomplish numerous tasks with ease.

"Distinctly David Fodero," they remarked at the same time.

"David doesn't title his artworks." Julian pointed to the top of the canvas.

"He used to, probably for cataloguing and sales purposes." She dismissed Julian's observation with a shrug. "Not anymore, though. His art is so unique people recognize his work immediately."

"Notice the dog." Julian set the pitcher on her table and edged his finger along the strong lines of a tiny dachshund in the upper right-hand corner.

"David inserts minute details a casual observer might miss." Ashley folded the cloth napkin on her lap. "However, the bold yellow and orange tints of the wildflowers stand out."

"He pushes boundaries. When I first saw his work, he was painting everyday objects and enhancing them."

"Such as?"

"The sides of a barn painted lime green. Daffodils were growing out of the roof."

"He still paints the everyday objects, only now his paintings are more intricate."

Julian hesitated. "You're an artist?"

"No." Ashley smiled at his question. "I own an art studio for handicapped children in Greenwood. My studio is connected to a café and an art gallery run by a friend. She has sold quite a few of David's works, including his lithographs."

"He moved to Cherish a few months ago, but I haven't seen much of him. When we talk, I brag about the advantages of living in a close-knit town where faith emboldens the residents."

Ashley grinned. "What's his response?"

"He replies with a noncommittal shrug." Julian brushed an invisible speck off her linen tablecloth. "All we can provide is prayer and trust God to show David the right direction."

"I've perfected worrying, and I worry about David."

"Why?"

"He's remarkably talented. Maybe too talented." She paused, frowning at her reply, conscious it made no sense. She chose not to divulge David's vision loss in case Julian was unaware.

He studied the painting further. "Everyone in the community is thrilled he decided to live here."

"An acclaimed artist who fled the center of the art universe when he reached the pinnacle of his career."

"New York City's loss. Cherish's gain."

Her server set down her appetizer, which had been recommended—sweet and sour meatballs.

Ashley bowed her head to say grace, then helped herself to a meatball. "Delicious." She dabbed a smear of sweet sauce from her chin.

"All the credit goes to Melissa, our magnificent cook. Her secret ingredient is orange marmalade." Julian threw a satisfied glance toward the kitchen. "I understand David hasn't completely cut his ties to New York. He still owns a penthouse on Central Park."

Ashley nodded. "I remember seeing photos. Glass-wrapped and two full floors, with a whopping eight thousand square feet of space."

Julian glanced at the New York guidebook Ashley had set on the table. "Have you ever visited Manhattan?"

"Never, though it's on my list of places to see."

"If David felt the need for a change of scenery, I guess it makes sense that he decided to buy a cabin here. I hear he did extensive renovations. Rumor is the place is a stunner."

She nodded. Her lips quirked in a smile. What she'd seen of David's place was stunning, with a distinctly masculine vibe.

"Once in a while," Julian added, "he breezes in for a takeout meal."

"He never dines in the restaurant?"

"No." Julian turned to an unoccupied table, fine-tuning the glassware. "He seems a good guy the few times we've spoken. He's generous to the shopkeepers and an excellent tipper. He donated his artwork to various businesses including a silent auction for Canine Helpers, a volunteer organization that supports veterans, and his piece raised thousands of dollars. When word of his contributions spread, tourism will surely increase."

"Which would be great for Cherish. It's such a quaint and charming town."

"I agree. I first came here a few years ago to supervise the opening of a new restaurant. I expected to stay only a few months, but I ended up meeting the woman of my dreams. Now, we're married and I'm helping raise Samantha, my precocious stepdaughter. She recently turned twenty."

"I met her at breakfast. She is lovely."

"She is musically talented, as well." Julian beamed, then fired a glance at a waitress displaying an assortment of desserts to an older couple who hadn't yet finished their meal.

"What's the name of the new restaurant?" Ashley bit into another meatball, savoring the tasty blend.

"Fresh 'n' Good, and it isn't new anymore. You may have seen the building." Julian's gaze swung to another waitress who attempted to balance too many entrees on a single tray. He stepped over to assist.

"I haven't had time to explore the town," Ashley said when he returned, "although I'm familiar with the chain."

"The restaurant is near the train station and was a former shoe store. I like to think we're friendly competition. Keeps both of our restaurants on our toes." He grinned. "Get it? Toes? Shoes?"

"Clever." Ashley laughed and turned toward the enormous picture window overlooking the street. The night sky glowed with the lights from the town. Traffic was easy—a brown Jeep and an old-fashioned Volkswagen drove by. At the intersection was a gas station attached to a bustling diner. When she had checked in the day before, Julian had told her that men sat there for hours solving the world's troubles, and coffee was poured nonstop.

"The town is growing, yet Cherish remains a faithful community honoring God," Julian said. He gave her an inquisitive glance. "What brings you here, besides the wonderful accommodations, religion, and delicious food?"

She grinned. "Wonderful accommodations?"

He actually puffed out his chest. "Tried, tested, and true."

She smirked. "Sarah Archer and I met at a mutual friend's wedding a few years ago."

"I know her and her husband well."

"We stay in touch through phone calls and emails and wanted to catch up in person."

There was more, a lot more, but Ashley couldn't divulge anything else to this gracious innkeeper.

"Samantha and I play a game." Julian shifted their conversation. "Whenever we see a David Fodero original, we try to describe it in two words."

"You narrow his complicated pieces down to two words?" Ashley considered the idea, staring down at her water glass. "It's not possible."

"Sure it is. My turn first. Radical and imaginative."

"Not fair. You've had loads of practice." She lifted her glass to salute him. "Scenic and surreal."

39

"Excellent." He reached for the water pitcher and waved down a waitress balancing another dessert tray. "David painted that landscape when he first moved to town and brought it here one afternoon. He insisted I hang it wherever I wished."

"And you wished to hang it on a prominent wall in your restaurant."

"Why not? I'm a businessman and publicity is publicity." Julian grinned, held up a hand to the waitress and mouthed, "I'm coming."

Ashley nodded at the painting. "Where is the place David painted?"

"Close. So close, in fact, you can walk there. When you reach Memorial Street Church, go a little farther and you'll see an abandoned rail line bordered by a river."

"I'll check it out."

"Are you an art lover?"

She contemplated her answer, choosing to be 100 percent honest. "Actually, I'm the planet's most enthusiastic fan."

Especially of David Fodero, she amended to herself.

CHAPTER 4

Inspiration does exist, but it must find you working.
- Picasso

When the sun rose the following morning, Ashley considered checking out the work-out room, but then decided to wait another day. Instead, she showered and washed her hair with lemon-scented shampoo, then chose a pair of cotton tie-dyed shorts and a chambray button-up top. After a quick breakfast to spoon a container of yogurt and drink a cup of sugary coffee, she exited the inn. She couldn't resist pausing on the front porch to rock back and forth on one of the inn's wide-slatted rocking chairs before heading to the town square.

She picked up a basket of ripe peaches from the farmer's market, inhaling whiffs of buttered popcorn and spun sugar, and treated herself to an herbal lavender tea served in a miniature paper cup.

She decided to bring the peaches to David's cabin as a

gesture of gratitude for his hospitality. Sure, it was an excuse to speak with him further, though she couldn't explain away the urge to see him again so soon.

David. She smiled just thinking about him.

Polite but distant, he'd offered to help with her car. She well remembered the quirk of his dark eyebrows when he'd remarked on Grandfather Mountain being located in North Carolina. His chuckle had been deep, holding good-natured amusement.

She must come clean with him, and soon. Still, she hesitated. She suspected David didn't appreciate dishonesty.

Slow. Think it through. Use finesse. And pray.

She tramped back to the inn, then drove to the town's outskirts. Following the exit that led to the state park, she soon sighted Pine Knoll Lane. She parked in front of David's cabin and followed the stepping-stone path to the door.

With a rapid knock, she called out, "Anyone home?"

She peered around. No dog bark from Pickle, and David's green pickup truck wasn't in the driveway. She peeked through the expansive bay window. The living room looked the same—neat and orderly, with assorted canvases, paints, brushes, and a metal tray stacked and sorted.

She tried the handle, surprised when the door opened. Fearful the fruit wouldn't tolerate the heat well, she set the basket on the foyer floor. A glimpse of the distinctive redwood chair prompted her to peek further inside.

The entryway led to the living room. Beyond, a full bathroom and a study. A wooden desk was cluttered with art books, and a laptop computer sat closed. A layer of dust begged for a housekeeper, and she had the sense he must employ someone once in a while. As she doubled back to the living room, a sleek black metal spiral staircase beckoned.

No. Too personal.

Should she? She twisted her hands, then craned her neck

42

upward. No, she shouldn't, but she couldn't resist. Quickly, she mounted the steps. An upstairs bedroom boasted a double bed with a wood paneled headboard and brown tweed comforter set. The air smelled of him—sandalwood and pine.

The room was neat and clean, the exception being a pair of jeans and a T-shirt draped over the bed. An elaborate sound system took up one corner, and a stack of audiobooks stood on a nearby shelf.

Odd that a man who painted such abstract art chose traditional décor for his personal space. It didn't fit his narrative, although nothing about David surprised her.

She retraced her steps downstairs, and the kitchen proved a shocker. Despite the meticulous renovations throughout the cabin, this room appeared untouched, as if taken straight from her grandmother's era.

She returned to the front door and grabbed a scrap of paper and a pen from her purse.

Sorry I missed you! I stopped by to thank you for the use of your phone. I hope to catch up with you soon.

Ashley Madden

She skimmed the note. Ugh. Had she mentioned her last name when she'd introduced herself? She couldn't remember.

Was the wording too forward? And what about the exclamation mark? She *was* sorry she missed him, but she didn't want him to suspect how much.

Well, she couldn't wipe out her message and begin again, as with an email. The note would have to suffice. She placed it with the peaches, closed the front door, and walked along the gravel driveway back to her car.

In the town center a while later, she wandered through the appealing boutiques, thrilled to discover David Fodero originals—quirky, fun and bold—in nearly every shop.

43

The owners all recounted the same tale when she inquired about the small canvases. David requested they not sell them but were free to display them. The paintings were gifts because he was pleased to be part of a caring community.

In Musically Yours, a music store in town, Ashley introduced herself to Dorothy Edwards, the owner. She was a spunky woman with emerald-green eyes and a slim figure. Dorothy was a pianist and her husband, Ryan, an opera singer.

"Please attend our outdoor concerts in the village park this summer." Dorothy gestured to a bulletin board tacked with the town's events.

"I'm only in Cherish for the week. I'm visiting."

"What brings you here?"

"A friend. You may know Sarah Archer?"

"Certainly. This is a tiny community. Her husband sings and plays harmonica in our church." Dorothy bobbed toward a mountain of sheet music on the counter. "The latest hymn arrangements just came in."

"I teach art to children, and also teach Sunday school."

"Art and music are closely related." The continuously busy Dorothy moved on to arrange a display of Percy Grainger statues, explaining that the store was celebrating the composer's birthday all month.

"I've never heard of him," Ashley confessed.

"Many people haven't, which is why we're spotlighting him. He was born in Australia and became an American citizen. Listen to his arrangements, especially 'Seventeen Come Sunday,' an English folk song. Or, his piano rendition of 'Country Gardens.' You'll recognize the tune."

Ashley's gaze returned to David's canvas behind the counter. "Outstanding. I can identify his paintings immediately."

"He presented the painting to me as a gift when he first moved here," Dorothy said as she filed a pile of Percy Grainger posters. "I got the impression he was subtly giving a message—he valued friendship but didn't want his privacy breached."

"Fair enough." Ashley's gaze skirted again to David's painting.

Nancy's art gallery displayed his larger canvases and sold them for several thousand dollars. Upon closer inspection, Ashley preferred his 8 x 10 inch, more intimate pieces— always with a hidden, or not-so-hidden dog in the upper right-hand corner.

She might even be able to afford one of his smaller works, and mentally redecorated her apartment, finding blank wall space where she could hang his paintings. However, they weren't for sale anymore, not in Greenwood, not in Cherish. Not anywhere.

She detoured to where David had painted the landscape he'd donated to the inn. She parked at Memorial Street Church and walked a short distance to an abandoned rail- way. The pavement glittered with the hotness of the midday sun.

After she worked her way through a narrow trail and reached a clearing, she didn't expect to encounter him. But there he was. In the same grove, surrounded by a kaleido- scopic array of wildflowers, with oak trees and a river beyond.

The air was scented with moss and earth, and the hint of summer blossoms.

She stared at him, open-mouthed, thrilled with her good fortune.

His heather gray T-shirt touting a well-known New York tourist attraction and slim-fitting Bermuda shorts enhanced his muscular physique. Again, he didn't fit her image of a reclusive painter.

But then, he wasn't painting. Rather, he was taking photographs, the camera slung around his neck by a strap, a tripod beside him.

She approached him from behind, on his right side, and he didn't seem conscious of her until she stepped in front of him. Or perhaps because his dog raced over with welcoming barks and sturdy tail wagging.

David looked wildly around and raked the dark hair from his forehead. The skin bunched at the corner of his eyes. "Ashley Madden. I didn't see you at first."

"Hello, David." Her heart shouldn't tingle because he'd uttered her name. And why wasn't there a sense of strangeness? They'd only just met.

"Sorry," she went on. "I didn't mean to come up on you so quietly." She stepped back while inwardly reprimanding herself. She'd been inconsiderate for advancing on him without warning.

He ran a thumb across his camera. "When I'm involved in my work, I'm focused and block out everything else."

She couldn't ignore the pride on his handsome face when he'd recovered from being startled by her approach. Surely a man like him never succumbed to weakness or defeat. Clearly, he hadn't seen her, though he'd object to anyone feeling sorry for him. Still, he needed support and morale boosting from someone.

And who might that someone be?

Nope. Not going there.

Sure, he was talented, an animal lover, and definitely generous.

And she'd begun to daydream about him, although she stifled any romantic notions. Nevertheless, she was drawn to him.

"How did you come upon these broken-down railroad tracks?" He grinned. "The running train is located on the opposite side of town."

"I'm not going anywhere." She smiled from ear to ear. "Today, I'm discovering Cherish."

He set the camera on a stool beside him. "You're still looking for Grandfather Mountain?"

"Grandfather Mountain? Why would I—"

"Remember? You're a mountain climber."

A glimpse of his boyish grin, more relaxed now, and she forgot her reasons for anything besides him.

"Grandfather Mountain is a distinctive mountain in the Blue Ridge Range," she informed him. As soon as she'd gone back to her room, the first day she met him, she'd done her research on the internet.

"How tall is it?"

"What is this? *Jeopardy?*"

"Just asking."

"Five thousand, nine hundred, and forty-six feet."

"Excellent." He laced the word with teasing amusement. "What other mountains do you climb?"

She bunched her hands into her pockets. "I stick to the basics."

"Basic mountains?"

"I'm referring to my gear."

"I assume you bring a rope, climbing pack, helmet and a harness."

She fumbled for the right words. "Yes, and a ... a headlamp." Once, she'd watched a television documentary about a mountain climber and he'd used a headlamp.

David feigned absorption in the rushing river behind her. Yet when he met her gaze, she caught a glimpse of unaffected warmth in his blue eyes.

47

"A climbing headlamp is useful after sundown," he suggested helpfully.

"A super bright lamp is crucial." She stalled, searching her mind for helpful details, counting on someone, anyone, who might appear and come to her rescue. In the end, it was David.

He moved closer. "You don't know all that much about mountain climbing, do you?"

"An understatement to say the least." She scooped up Pickle, who rewarded her with a dozen licks to her chin. "How did you guess my secret?"

"Call me a regular Sherlock Holmes. Or maybe it was the headlamp reference." Lightly, he brushed his knuckles over her cheek, disarming her. "I'm just messing with you. I don't know anything about mountain climbing, either."

"I'm ignorant when it comes to mountain ranges too."

"Well, you could've fooled me." He seemed to try his best not to look surprised. "By the way, someone broke into my house today."

"Huh."

"Huh? Meaning?"

"It was me." She held up a hand. "Although to clarify, I didn't break in because the door was unlocked. Plus, I had an excellent reason."

"I can only imagine." He waited, shifted. "Go on."

"I was worried about ... about the peaches."

"I wasn't aware peaches had feelings."

"The heat is excessive, and the peaches were already ripe when I bought them at the farmer's market. I feared they might spoil. Your doorstep gets a lot of sun."

"You're blaming your break-in on my sunny doorstep?"

"It wasn't a break-in," she clarified, straightening her shoulders. "But yes, it's all your fault."

"Well, that explains everything." His laughter rang out,

and the last bit of tension vanished from his face. "Thanks for the treat. They're delicious. I already ate two."

"You're welcome."

"What made you decide on peaches?" He shifted to face her. "They're my favorite fruit."

"Peaches were a wild guess, though they're in season and I assumed everyone likes them." She set Pickle down. He lapped up the water in his dish and found a shady spot in the grass beneath an oak tree. "Thanks again."

"Glad to oblige." David's smile was candid. "Next time we'll devour a box of cookies and drink sugary soda."

Next time? She muffled a self-conscious laugh while her heart skipped a beat.

She stepped over to the tree and crouched to give Pickle a belly rub. The dog rolled onto his back, feet splayed to provide better access to his stomach.

"Did you peek through my house while you were inside today?" he asked.

"Snoop?"

"Peek, snoop ..."

"Neither is flattering. I was in and out quickly. *Fairly quickly,* she amended, sending a prayer to God. In retrospect, it had been an intrusion on David's personal space.

God is within me. God is rooting for me. Focus on His word and God, please forgive me.

Now was a suitable time to explain to David why she was really in Cherish. But he was smiling, and the mood was congenial. She didn't want to spoil it.

"You mentioned you're not from around here," he said.

"I live in a town fifty miles away."

"Not far."

"Not far. It's similar in size and population to Cherish, though Cherish has more of a quintessential..."

"Charm?"

"The optimal description."

He waited, apparently, for her to continue.

"I own an art studio for handicapped children. I allow my students the freedom to create art in any form they choose. There's no right or wrong."

"Admirable." He yanked open a portable cooler at his feet and offered her a bottle of root beer and an almond biscuit from a bakery in town, which she gratefully accepted. He grabbed an energy drink for himself.

"The soda isn't sugar free." All the while, his gaze stayed on her. "Neither is the biscuit."

"Best news of the day."

He laughed. "I assume your teaching is challenging?"

"My students are a pleasure, and my studio is a work in progress. I love sharing the beauty and wonder of art."

He transferred his weight from one foot to the other. "Why are you here in Cherish?"

She blinked, caught by his question, scarcely able to breathe because of his closeness. "I'm searching for distinctive art supplies to stock my studio."

Actually, she was in Cherish because of the tall, handsome man eyeing her with undisguised interest.

He reached for another biscuit. "Aaron's Art is an excellent shop in town."

"I'll stop by while I'm here."

"I can show you sometime."

She answered with a surprised smile. "I'll take you up on your offer."

She tried to ignore the leap of her pulse at the sight of David's dazzling grin. He gave a thumbs-up.

"Do you pay for your studio items out of your own pocket?" he asked.

"Of course, although I charge minimal tuition." An abrupt

memory of the many months when she'd scarcely been able to pay the heat and electric bills flashed through her mind. "Sometimes, I receive donations from my church, which is a huge help."

"If you ever need anything, I own a warehouse in New York filled with supplies."

"Thank you. I'm always running out of metal buckets and paint brushes and canvases. It's all worth it, though. Art is healing."

"Exactly." He treated her with a mixture of courtesy and sincerity. There was a guarded attentiveness from this urbane, handsome man. She couldn't shake the feeling he sensed their growing attraction, too.

He uncapped his energy drink. "What else do you provide for your students?"

"Unconditional love and support."

"There's nothing better." His gaze, shining with respect, met hers. "You're staying at the Cherish Hills Inn?"

"Yes. I booked a room for the next few days. The owner is accommodating, and the food is fabulous." She paused, the biscuit in her hand temporarily forgotten.

Nerves kicked in. Why was he asking? Was he interested in her? In a sense, he'd asked her out by offering to show her the art shop. And he'd mentioned sharing cookies.

"Julian is a hands-on owner, and his cook, Melissa, produces marvelous dishes."

Thinking of her exquisite meal the night before, she nodded. "The restaurant offers top-notch service. I enjoyed dinner there, and the sweet and sour meatballs are scrumptious."

"You ate alone?" David asked. He finished his second biscuit and drank half his energy drink.

"I'm single and usually eat by myself."

Something stirred in the immeasurable depths of his eyes. Something warm. "I prefer to dine with a beautiful companion."

Judging from photos she'd seen of him through the years, there was often a glamorous starlet hanging from his arm. Ashley swallowed, torn between awkwardness and self-consciousness. She was neither stunning nor a starlet.

The warmth in his eyes was replaced by an emotion she couldn't pinpoint. And then he became unreadable.

"In all honesty," he said, shoving his hands into his pockets. "I'm surprised."

"Why?"

"A breathtaking woman like you should've been snatched up long ago."

"I'm a seasoned solo diner with no romantic commitments. I'm also a foodie."

"I eat by myself more often than not."

Her eyes widened. She couldn't imagine him dining alone. "Do you prefer it?"

"Not a bit."

She smiled. "When dining in a restaurant, the secret is to take along props."

"A fork and a spoon?"

She choked on a laugh. "A travel book is good. I recommend *The Lonely Planet*."

"Where do you travel?"

"Nowhere, though I've always wanted to tour Italy, particularly the Campania region and Naples."

"I've visited. The word *scenic* doesn't capture Italy's breathtaking coastlines. Traveling is my passion, and that country is a favorite."

"I've read that every meal in Italy is a memorable experience."

"Tuscany resembles something straight out of a picture book."

Now they had Italy in common, besides art and a love of animals.

"When dining alone ..." She paused for a dramatic effect. "I pull up the e-reader on my phone."

"How about taking a companion with you to dinner?"

Her eyebrows raised, along with her spirit. She couldn't be certain if he was flirting, but elected to participate. "Do you have anyone in mind?"

"Me, because I haven't eaten there yet."

"I heard you frequently order takeout." She prayed she wasn't initiating a topic too prying, but took the dive, anyway. "Julian Wilson mentioned it last night."

A sparkle lit his eyes as he placed a hand on her shoulder. "I'm the center of a conversation?"

Her mouth went dry. She swallowed. Truth? These days, he was the center of all her conversations. All her thoughts.

She dismissed his teasing query with a chuckle. "You were worth a quick mention."

"Thanks for letting me down gently." He granted her a rueful smile. His hand leisurely massaged her shoulder. "Hence, will you?"

"Hence? Will I ...Wait. Are you asking me out to dinner, or am I asking you?"

A softness shone from his blue eyes. His eyes, she decided, were designed to mesmerize. She couldn't look away.

"To clarify, I'm asking you. I hope you'll accept." His hand remained on her shoulder, and the chemistry between them heated. He realized it, too. She heard the evidence from the tenderness in his tone.

"You're splashed on the front page of gossip newspapers

with models and actresses—" Ashley stopped herself. Whoa. This chat was becoming overly personal.

"Gossip newspapers don't reveal a factual story. Many of those women simply craved publicity. I was the man of the hour, though insincerity isn't my thing." The edginess vanished from his voice, replaced with a hint of gratefulness. "The woman of my dreams has a sense of humor and is a delight to be around."

"I've never dated anyone famous."

He rubbed his forehead. "Why bring up that particular word at this precise minute?"

"Because I'm the opposite of your usual choice in women."

His gaze narrowed. "You're an authority on me in the short time we've known each other?"

"You mentioned insincerity wasn't your thing," she continued. "I'd welcome the same consideration."

"You don't believe I'm sincere?"

"I don't know you well enough to determine either way."

"So I'm guilty."

"I didn't say that."

She had, though.

Too late, she noticed his troubled expression, and regretted allowing her emotions to steer her toward such a blunt outburst. She braced herself for a verbal lambasting, but after a blink of silence, he replied, "I value your honesty. You're a refreshing change in my jaded world."

She drew in a breath and didn't meet his gaze.

Her conscience tapped her on the shoulder. Insincerity? She was the one being dishonest. What about the bigger explanation of her sudden appearance in Cherish?

"Ashley?" David's tone was just enough of a caress that she ignored her conscience. Though if he was extending a genuine invitation, she wasn't sure how to respond. She only knew she was pleased and thrilled and welcomed the excitement seeping through her body.

"Yes?"

"I'm sincere." His gaze dropped to her mouth.

In a state of expectation, she waited for him to kiss her. When it proved apparent after awkward seconds passed that he hadn't planned any such thing, she disguised her disappointment beneath a luminous smile.

"I'll accept your dinner invitation under one condition," she replied.

"Which is?"

"Cookies are on the dessert menu."

"Any particular kind? Frozen, I assume?"

She chuckled. "I have an affinity for chocolate. Frozen is incomparable. Thawed is acceptable."

"I'm certain the innkeeper can arrange chocolate cookies to your liking." David burst out laughing, then pressed a fleeting kiss to her forehead.

She tipped up her chin. "What's that for?"

"The laugh or the kiss?"

"The kiss."

His admiring gaze roved over her from head to toe. "My kiss is expressing gratitude for keeping me on track. For granting me the unexpected freedom to laugh out loud. For looking incredibly enchanting in a simple outfit of shorts and a chambray blouse."

That described her to a T. Simple. Not striking. Not glamorous.

Simple.

His compliment was nothing more than lighthearted flattery. She gazed past him at the spectacular scene of mountains and sky far beyond the crystal-clear river.

He chucked her under the chin and the romantic moment, if that was indeed what it had been, eased.

He nodded toward the stool and gestured for her to sit.

She threw him a questioning glance. "But there's only one stool."

"And it's for you." An amused sparkle lit his eyes as he leaned against a tree. "Unless you'd like to share it."

Rather than disagree, she sat as he requested, and set the soda beside her, leaving no space for him. She was certain her cheeks had heated to a flushed pink that had little to do with the warmth of the day, and more to do with the good-looking man standing a few feet away.

"You asked a lot about me," she said, "but why are you in town, David?"

"I'm here on Marge Addyson's invitation. I was commissioned to paint a portrait for the centennial celebration of Memorial Street Church." He grabbed a third biscuit, thoughtfully chewed, then drained his energy drink. "Marge is the associate pastor, my benefactor, and a kind, thoughtful woman. Based on her request, the artwork will be personalized with a then and now quality."

"Two paintings?"

"I haven't decided. Perhaps two-sided art, or two renderings of the church, the older version drawn in charcoal."

"On the same canvas?"

"Maybe."

"I'm certain anything you paint will be marvelous."

"Let's settle on acceptable."

Her heart skipped a beat at the uncertainty in his expression. If she hadn't glanced up, she would've missed it, so fleeting had it crossed his face.

She groped for an upbeat topic. "Do you intend to live in Cherish permanently?"

"I signed a contract."

"For the commission or the cabin?"

"The commission, which is to be delivered the final week of August. I purchased the cabin outright."

Mentally, she gauged the price. With David's extensive renovations, she estimated a cost of at least a half million dollars.

"I'm single with no ties," he went on. "I wanted a discreet out-of-the-way house. When I first visited, this town fit the bill. The right place, the right season in my life."

She hung onto the beginning of his sentence. "Why?"

"Why I'm not married? I'm only thirty-five. There's still time." He rubbed his eyes. "I suppose the first reason is because no woman seemed interested in dating a starving artist."

"You're hardly starving anymore."

"I was dirt-poor for many years." His eyes shuttered, a sharpness carried his tone. "You've heard of overnight successes?"

"Hasn't everyone?"

"Whatever you're inclined to believe, there is no such thing. Almost 100 percent of anyone who has achieved any semblance of success worked hard to get there."

"You mentioned a first reason." Ashley rounded on him. "Is there a second?"

"Second what?"

"Second reason you're not married."

"I never allow a relationship to last over the three-month line." He rubbed his temples. "I found it's easier that way. No one gets hurt."

She fixed her stare on the tranquil scene of wildflowers and water and a sleeping dog. He'd certainly given her something to mull over.

David picked up his camera, slung the strap around his neck, then began taking photos. He used his left eye to focus.

"I'm left-eye dominant too." She stood and stepped to an

oak tree near the river. "Most people are right-eye dominant."

No answer, only more camera clicks.

"Gorgeous and natural," he murmured.

She surveyed the base of the tree. "Do you fish?"

"Nope."

"There's certainly access to fishing in this town."

"Yup."

Pickle woke, stretched, then dozed again.

"Will you use these photos as a reference to reproduce on canvas?" She anchored her foot on the lowest branch of the tree.

A fair question, though again, David didn't respond. Instead, he stepped back and muttered something about tight and wide shots.

She squinted up at the sun. "What's the ideal light for outdoor photography?"

"It depends on what I'm shooting."

She curled her fingers around the next tree branch, testing to be certain it would hold her weight, then scrambled to the sturdy upper limb.

He swiveled toward her, open-mouthed. "What are you doing?"

"I'm climbing a tree."

"I'm quite aware." His lips quirked. "May I ask why?"

"So I can sit."

"There are stools for the same purpose."

"I see better up here."

"Isn't that a bit childish?"

"I'm an adult, but it doesn't mean I should give up everything I loved to do when I was young. The view is different up here. Better. I can see beyond the river to the grassy knoll bordering the mountains." At his curious look, she added, "Haven't you ever climbed a tree?"

"When I was ten."

"What was it like?"

He blinked and averted his gaze. "I climbed an old maple tree higher and higher. Then I looked down."

"And?"

"I closed my eyes and gasped for oxygen. When I opened them, I was sweating profusely."

"What happened next?"

"I lost my balance and fell out of the tree."

"Oh, no." She clung tighter to a skinny branch. "I hope you weren't hurt."

"Only my pride." He gazed up at her. "My brothers thought it was the funniest thing they'd seen in a decade. They laughed for days."

"Did you ever try again?"

"Nope. Do I look like a fool?"

"Chicken."

Her prim correction brought a chuckle. Then a sigh. Then another series of clicks as he lifted his camera.

"How many shots do you usually take?" she called down to him.

"Thirty or forty." His manner was preoccupied. "I file my photographs in an image library."

"All part of the creative process." She shifted to a different branch. "I've learned that subject is most important in art and photography."

Again, he placed the camera close to his eye and took aim at the river. "And in life."

His statement, his philosophy, she wasn't sure.

She looped strands of hair slipping loose from her ponytail behind her ear. She repeated to herself that she was in Cherish for a purpose, to discuss if he planned to sell his artwork anymore. Equally important, he should consult an eye doctor.

Perhaps he already had. He certainly had the financial resources.

Should she ask? Wouldn't that be prying into his personal affairs?

And why couldn't she keep her gaze off him for longer than half a second?

By now she had surmised he was losing, or perhaps had lost, total vision in his right eye. He was discernibly uncomfortable discussing the subject, though he'd alluded to the eyesight loss in his cabin. Just as easily, he had shut the discourse down before she'd uttered a word. He had a knack for dictating a conversation.

Another stretch of silence. She climbed down from the tree, reached for her soda and took a sip. The drink was warm, and flat.

When she brought up how summer colds were sometimes worse than winter colds, citing various reasons, David teased her about being a regular Dr. Google.

Then, she focused on the wildflowers.

"They're exquisite, aren't they?" she rhapsodized. "I especially love red and pink. The shades are vibrant."

"Yup," came his reply.

Not much of a response. Artists realized the power of color, and she'd taught her students that color brought out emotions. She recommended vibrant, cool, warm, and complementary paint in every piece her students created.

When she had exhausted any further attempts about uncontroversial subjects—the weather, various dog breeds, favorite television shows—hers was the *Andy Griffith Show*, David packed his camera and tripod in a brown leather messenger bag. He expelled a breath, hoisted the bag over his shoulder, and leashed Pickle.

"Are you headed to the inn, Ashley?" He glanced at his watch and frowned. "I'm giving up for today."

"Giving up what?"

"Work, photographs, art. Nothing is cooperating, including the weather."

"Why? Is it supposed to rain?" She caught his frown, then raised her gaze to the heavens. As if the mention of rain had conjured up the finale of a picture-perfect sky, clouds had begun to form.

"Nothing in the forecast, and the weather is warm but pleasant." He cut off any further questions by stating, "It's getting late."

Four o'clock in the afternoon was hardly late for two grown adults. Tree branches swayed in the breeze, and squirrels scampered from tree to tree.

She scowled at her flat soda. Suddenly, David had become aware of her again.

"As a matter of fact, I am headed to the inn," she said.

"I can walk you there."

Was he sincere or offering out of courtesy?

Around him, her thoughts became increasingly tangled. She felt like she was on a roller coaster—thrilling, adrenaline-filled, and exhilarating when he was near. At other times, the hours slowed, and she could hardly catch a breath.

Both instances had the same common denominator.

Him.

An hour ago, they seemed in perfect accord. Presently, she was trying her best to ignore the blow to her pride by his sudden memory loss. Had he forgotten he'd suggested they have dinner together?

"I'm fully aware of the inn's location," she said. "I don't require an escort to walk a few short blocks." She sought to sound indifferent and knew she didn't when the words trapped in her throat.

Nonetheless, she didn't appreciate the way he'd dismissed her.

Typical difficult artist.

"Besides," she added, "my car is parked a short distance from here." She offered a grim smile. "Thanks anyway. Good day, David."

Later, she'd wonder how she pulled off ending the conversation with such supreme self-confidence. She kept her posture straight, whirled on her heel, and marched away.

CHAPTER 5

Every act of creation is first of all an act of destruction.
– Picasso

*H*ours later, David shook his head. *Wow, had he bungled that badly.*

When he and Ashley had stood near the oak tree, he'd watched her delicate eyebrows knit together in a frown before she'd stomped away. Contrary to his expectation she'd accept his offer to walk her to the inn, she'd done the opposite.

It was his fault.

She'd given such a jaunty declaration that she knew where the inn was, that he'd wanted to take her in his arms and kiss her soft, full lips.

Standing by the window in his cabin, he gazed out at the night sky. The slender leaves of willow oaks flickered under the silver light cast by a quarter moon. He stared blindly at

63

his reflection and raked a hand through his messy shag, begging for a haircut.

He braced an arm on the frame and surveyed the last of the clouds. Despite the forecast, it had rained earlier. He opened the window to allow the breeze to wash a freshness through the room.

He hardly knew how to cope with the range of emotions he was experiencing.

An attractive, charming woman had expressed interest in his paintings, perhaps in him, and he'd been less than enthusiastic. He reprimanded himself over the unfairness of taking his frustration over his lost eyesight out on her, but he hadn't been able to see into the camera as easily as he'd anticipated. He'd been in the zone initially, snapping photos intuitively and envisioning them. Exhilaration and enthusiasm had pressed him to continue. Soon, he'd questioned himself as he realized he couldn't identify subjects as clearly as he liked.

In addition, he'd felt disheartened when Ashley had remarked on his fame.

If anything, he felt like a failure. Sure, he'd spent his entire adulthood beneath the celebrity umbrella, but the mention always made him uncomfortable.

Was that all she saw in him?

He wasn't an award for a woman to parade on her arm. He was a living, breathing man, not a slicked-up magazine cover. Similar to newsworthy men in the public eye—movie stars and prominent sport figures—his tranquility had been invaded by women fascinated not by him nor his art, but by the prospect of enlisting him as their escort for popular media events.

Not the man. Not him.

Rather, how the reclusive, mysterious artist might bolster their career.

The afternoon with Ashley was the first time he believed

a woman was drawn to him solely for himself. He'd learned a little about her and had been captivated by her kind-heartedness and ideals. She was a breath of pure air, and refreshingly uninterested in money and power.

Thus, he was surprised he'd been wrong about her.

But no, no, he wasn't wrong. He'd recognized the interest in her gorgeous hazel eyes whenever she gazed up at him.

Something was happening between them. Something special. Something magnetic.

While he'd taken photos of the landscape and river, he'd caught her staring at him from the corner of his good eye. Involuntarily, he'd begun to memorize her face—all pink-cheeked and beautiful and captivating.

His feelings were utterly illogical. He'd just met her. Nevertheless, the upsetting emotional and physical unbalances he'd faced because of his eyesight, coupled with the hours in her charming company, had merged together.

The result was excitement, a kind of euphoria he'd never experienced before.

The result was chaos. His reaction and judgement weren't functioning clearly.

Part of the time, he had the wildest sensation that she couldn't possibly be as genuine as she seemed. Vivacious and enchanting and embracing life, she brought to mind an eighteen-year-old girl on the verge of becoming a woman.

On the other hand, she made him feel like he was eighteen again, for she remained constantly in his thoughts.

He'd been sincere in his suggestion to walk her to the inn, hoping to prolong their afternoon together. It wasn't a big shock she refused. Why would she want to converse with someone like him, so sulky and self-absorbed?

"Ashley, Ashley." He whispered her name aloud.

Ideal on a marquee, definitely traditional, and beyond compare.

And her other name: *Twinkle.*

Why had her friend called her that?

Ashley had ignored his inquisitive stare at the time, though he intended to ask her the meaning of the nickname. She was an enigma he wanted to get to know better, and so he'd absorbed every word she'd uttered when they were together.

The first day they met, they'd shaken hands. Hers was dainty, like the woman herself, her fingers slim and firm. When she'd slipped off her sunglasses, she'd afforded him a glimpse of her startling eyes. Fascinating. Hazel eyes were set apart from brown or blue eyes because of their combination of green, gold, and brown.

She embodied the ideal subject—great cheekbones, finely arched eyebrows, and rounded, subtle features.

When Sarah and Ashley had readied to leave his cabin, he hadn't anticipated spouting about deaf musicians and blind painters. He'd just blurted it out. Shock and disbelief had flashed across Ashley's face.

She was considerate and compassionate. Her face lit up when she chatted about her students.

He closed the window, nodding quiet approval for her tender spirit.

When they'd stood by the river, her breath had quickened. He had wanted to kiss her, though he'd been uncertain if the timing was right. They were in the earliest stages of a relationship, slowly learning about each other. His heart had skipped a beat at her disappointed expression when he hadn't kissed her.

Taken aback by his next thought, he sighed. Why was he unsure about kissing her when every instinct told him it was right?

Why? Because he wasn't clear about anything anymore.

He glanced at Pickle, sleeping on a rug by the fireplace.

"Can you understand this relationship any better than I can?" he asked.

The living room lamps were on. The dog didn't respond, just continued sleeping with his legs extended. Pickle could sleep just about anywhere.

David closed his eyes and went over their afternoon again.

In addition to all the reasons he was intrigued by Ashley, she also liked his paintings and championed him. Her open praise was a welcome switch from his inner harsh criticism. Perhaps he should lighten up on himself.

THE NEXT DAY, David assessed the photographs he'd taken. Surprised, he sorted numerous shots with Ashley in them. He hadn't realized he'd included her. He hadn't been able to see her clearly whenever she stepped to his right and hadn't noticed her in his viewfinder.

Or had his subconscious known she was there all along?

Maybe...

He printed the best photos, assessed them, and chose one with her sitting in the tree, a suggestion of a fairy. She had shifted toward the water, and her profile—small, turned-up nose and lifted chin—created a fetching picture. The sun gilded her blond hair to a honey gold, her shapely legs were long and tanned, her creamy complexion sprinkled with freckles.

She'd glanced at him. He'd caught her expressive gaze, her lips poised in a smile. Rosy-red, her lower lip was fuller than her upper lip. Her chin was smooth, her cheeks velvety and dimpled. Yet he couldn't ignore the strength in her features.

Deprived of rational thinking, he'd captured her in a reflective, relaxed pose. Against the natural backdrop, Ashley Madden proved the ideal focus for a painting. Flawless.

67

Could he paint her from the photos without her permission?

Meeting her, capturing her exquisiteness…

Circumstances or all a coincidence?

He brought the photos into the kitchen. Well aware the kitchen was the main room to tackle when renovating an old house, he'd spent an afternoon listening to a builder explain traffic patterns, heating, plumbing lines, the latest "must-have's," and had opted to wait. He didn't need glass-fronted cabinets, stainless-steel appliances, or a marble-topped island. He preferred the rustic charm of blue painted cabinets and a stone floor.

He sat at the vintage wooden baking unit he used as a table and laid out the photos.

Surprisingly, Julian's voice rang in his ears. Whenever David stopped at the inn for takeout, Julian extolled the advantages of living in Cherish, sometimes peppering David with questions about his faith. For Julian, it was of utmost importance that the residents remained steadfast in their unwavering belief in God.

Had these last few months been guided by God's divine hand? Or could he attribute it to fate—the unexplainable law of the universe—that had brought him and Ashley together?

He poured himself an energy drink, took a gulp, then slumped back on the antique chair. Ah, the adrenaline of caffeine. Just the ticket to spur his brain's neural activity and quicken his thought process.

The dog trotted over and rested at his feet.

He scooped Pickle onto his lap and stroked the silky fur.

Perhaps Cherish was where he'd find his greatest freedom. Perhaps he should allow former priorities the opportunity to escape. Be inspired by a fresh perspective. Let go.

Let go of what exactly? His painting? His beloved art?

He wasn't certain. He just knew the faint murmur in his

heart whispered the observation that what he needed might be directly in front of him.

Nope, nope, nope. His hand stilled. He gazed at the beamed wooden ceiling. Dating? Women? Faith? Too much struggle. Too much conflict. Too much difficulty.

He well remembered his strict religious upbringing—the drone of Sunday sermons by an aged pastor when his parents had dragged him to church as a boy. His mother's insistence he dress properly in beige pants and a blue polo shirt. Their gasps of horror when he declared the sermons boring. He was an adolescent when doubts about God and Christianity had taken hold.

He gave a sad, small laugh. At himself, at the universe.

Maybe the time had come to accept whatever God had in store for him.

You're joking, right?

He shook off his musings, set the dog down, and shoved to his feet, turning to the refrigerator. He pulled a box of cookies from the freezer.

When he bit into one, still frozen, the way Ashley liked them, reality intruded.

God had been absent for decades. God wasn't interested in a man like David—with faults more numerous than the number of paintings he'd painted through the years. Besides, he was too much of a skeptic to change his religious views.

With a decisive nod, he vowed to be more attentive to his art and less attentive to his thoughts about Ashley. Surely thinking about her shouldn't consume him.

Ashley.

Any artist would clamor to paint an enchanting woman with such expressive eyes. A woman with a lean, breathtaking figure and a face that conveyed tenderness and compassion.

She was fascinating, and he wished to see her again. With

his mind made up, he placed the cookies back in the freezer. It would be better if he and Ashley ate them together. Along with bottles of soda loaded with sugar.

TIME HAD SMOOTHED over Ashley's upset of the previous day over David's not-so-polite dismissal of her. A morning workout crossed her mind, but she quickly dismissed the idea. Instead, she chose to explore the town more. In order to rationalize her morning jaunt, she popped into Aaron's Art, the shop David had mentioned. She invariably needed supplies for her studio.

Aaron, the owner, a hunched-over fellow with a white curly beard that reminded her of sheep's wool, sang David's praises. David had come into his store, learned Aaron struggled to meet his monthly rent payments because business was slow, and paid for the store's new heating and air conditioning unit. He'd made all the arrangements and sent Aaron a check to cover six months' rent as well.

"He's beyond generous. It's a shame he's hidden himself away." Aaron crossed over to her. "He'll appear for a couple hours and is gone by the time anyone realizes he was around."

"He's certainly made his mark in the artistic community." She instantly regretted saying anything, because she could almost see Aaron's ears perk up.

He stepped over to a display of pencil pocket sets. "Haven't you heard? He keeps himself scarce because he's losing his eyesight." Aaron scribbled a sign: *Superb For Traveling*.

"Rumors spread like wildfire, don't they?" Ashley said.

Aaron fixed her with a level look. "Sometimes."

Not everyone knew about David's eyesight loss, she

wanted to tell Aaron. Only those who spent a lengthy amount of time with David would have figured it out.

Like her, for instance. She was fortunate to have shared hours with him. He was complex and charming and … impossible. She hadn't broached the eyesight subject with him because she didn't want to hinder his creativity. And it seemed as if he was always creating. Also, she didn't want to interrupt their time together with upsetting conversation.

She remembered the way his gaze had dropped to her lips, the warmth of his skin. She longed to run her fingers through his messy, disheveled hair. Did he realize his hair curled at the nape?

They'd stared at each other as if they were both waiting for something.

What, exactly?

He wasn't falling in love with her, nor was he about to declare an everlasting declaration of any kind.

Neither was she.

She had resolved to preserve her heart behind a sheltered and safe wall. Love wasn't a part of her future, and any fleeting thoughts of her and David had to be quickly squelched. With him, she'd keep things businesslike. Besides, she wasn't stunning and sophisticated or similar in any way to the women he apparently preferred.

Allow me my privacy was his philosophy, and the reason why he'd attempted to conceal his whereabouts in this idyllic community.

She picked up a framed watercolor of Venice, Italy, and then gazed out the shop's front window. Townsfolk cheerfully greeted each other as they strolled along the sidewalk. Children skipped, the seniors walked slower, arm in arm.

Cherish had a glow all its own.

The simple acts of fellowship should have made her

spirits soar. Instead, they plummeted because all that good cheer effectively took her back to David's suffering.

Hiding his loss under an unbreachable demeanor might be his way. Not hers. God had placed outward limits on David's body, but His inner blessings were greater. She promised to pray and believe and lean on God. She wanted to inspire David to do likewise.

She purchased pocket sets, pens, and pencils for her students and thanked Aaron, suppressing her dismay that she wasn't able to afford more expensive items. She could've used an assortment of mason jars, but would have to wait.

She passed a sign on the corner advertising a Renaissance Faire in a neighboring town. She'd always wanted to attend one, but never had the opportunity.

Perhaps this time?

Her imagination conjured the aroma of pork on a stick, or a steak and mushroom meat pie, and her stomach rumbled. The idea of escaping to a medieval world, outside of modern everyday life, held a sense of adventure and decent, old-fashioned fun.

But no, not this trip. David Fodero absorbed all of her attention.

AN HOUR LATER, Ashley had showered and changed into a yellow sundress that hugged her slim figure, a bold necklace featuring a golden sunflower and beige leather sandals. Before she forgot Dorothy's recommendation from the music store, she listened to Percy Grainger's performance of 'Country Gardens.' She read about the pianist's fascinating life, spending more time on it than she'd foreseen, as he was praised for his talent.

Another typically difficult artist, she smiled to herself.

By seven o'clock, she was perched on a stool in the inn's

72

lounge, sipping a tall glass of sweet iced tea, mulling over different ways to help David.

Julian greeted her with a smile as he wended between bistro tables. He held a tumbler overflowing with fresh-squeezed limeade. He'd expounded earlier that limeade was an inn specialty beverage because of the addition of fresh mint leaves.

"I heard you were here." He leaned against the stool opposite her. "I'm the messenger this evening. Someone in the parlor wants to see you."

"Is Sarah here?" She sat forward. "I thought we were having lunch together in a few days. I hope I didn't get the times mixed up."

"I assure you it's not Sarah." Julian chuckled. "I haven't seen her tonight."

Ashley half stood. "Who, then?"

Julian toasted her glass with his. His eyes sparkled with merriment. "I'm fairly certainly you'll recognize him immediately."

CHAPTER 6

Good artists copy, great artists steal.
– Picasso

Seated on an overstuffed sofa in the parlor of the Cherish Hills Inn, David set a bouquet of wild-flowers on the coffee table, and then rifled through a pile of periodicals. Particularly catching his interest was a gardening magazine, reminding him that he planned to start his vegetable garden. He needed to contact Ashley's friend, Sarah.

"Anything I can help you with, sir?" A pleasant woman whom he guessed to be in her sixties, with curly gray hair and red-rouged cheeks, all beams and buoyancy, wheeled a trolley cart stacked with beverages and snacks toward him.

"No thanks. I'm set." He held up the magazine as proof.

Optimism all around seemed to be a prerequisite for living in Cherish, along with its close cousins—positivity and religion.

He smiled at her, then feigned absorption in an article touting the optimum season to plant pumpkins seeds. He assumed it was the fall. He was wrong. In the Carolinas, early July was deemed best. He'd better get on it so he could harvest something he'd be able to swallow. Sarah had mentioned squash and carrots and... What was the last vegetable? Something green he'd certainly not eaten before, and which was probably tasteless.

When he finished the article, he looked around, cheered by the surroundings—a stacked rock fireplace, cornflower-blue tapestry rug, and gleaming oak wood floors. A shaft of late-day sunlight slanted through the front window. Outside, the sky blazed a magnificent tangerine-orange. In the distance, a dog barked.

He'd considered bringing Pickle with him, but was uncertain if dogs were allowed. From comments on the internet, he'd learned the inn's previous owner had banned dogs. He wasn't certain of Julian's stance.

Before he had left his cabin, he'd given Pickle a gnawing toy and his favorite striped elephant. He'd tuned his radio to a country station that would provide, the DJ assured him, easy listening for Pickle. As he'd left, a male singer was crooning about how much better life would be if he only had a boat.

David smiled. Country music was fun and all about emotions. He was fairly certain there were no cleverer lyrics on earth.

The tensions of the day had drained as he stepped outside his cabin and into the sultry June evening. The air was thick and heavy, and a five-minute rain shower hadn't cooled things off.

Shifting to the present, he sat back on the sofa and pulled out his cell phone. He'd invested in a doggie camera he'd stationed in his living room, and streamed to his phone.

75

Currently, Pickle was participating in his favorite activity: sleeping.

"David?"

Ashley entered the parlor, a surprised smile on her face. He pocketed his phone, picked up the bouquet, and sprang to his feet. Her yellow dress complemented her blond hair, which spilled over her shoulders in delicate waves. She dressed with a casual finesse, perfectly suiting her symmetrical features.

"Hi, Ashley." His admiring gaze glided from the top of her head to the tips of her manicured toes.

"Hello." She set a glass of iced tea on a side table, her movements elegant, yet tentative. She reminded him of a pretty summer posy, feminine and romantic.

"I assume your tea is weighted down with sugar." He groped for the ideal words, stronger words, funnier words, and hoped his humor was contagious.

"I take three teaspoons. What's your preference?"

He matched her cheerful response. "I survive on energy drinks. I work better at night, and they help me stay awake."

"Not very healthy."

"Said the pot calling the kettle black."

"You realize caffeine is addictive?"

His retort was a bark of laughter. "Moderate consumption is okay."

"Now who is Dr. Google?"

He half smiled. Somehow, she'd flipped the conversation, causing him to consider the amount of caffeine he drank each day. Caffeine elevated his mood and kept him more alert. However, there was a major shortcoming. He'd come to rely on the drinks.

She raised her glass. "I assume you're a health nut."

"Me?" He wasn't smiling anymore. He was laughing.

"But you are into vegetables." She gestured to the magazine he'd been reading. "Aren't you planting a garden featuring everyone's favorite vegetable, zucchini?"

Right. The vegetable he couldn't remember.

Animated buzzing of conversation filled the inn's hallway, and the chiming of the pendulum clock had recently sounded the hour.

"I'd prefer to plant coffee beans bursting with caffeine," he replied.

"And I'd plant chocolate candy bars."

He started toward her, stopping within inches.

She stared up at him. "I didn't expect to see you tonight."

"Yet here I am." Captivated, he focused on her amazing smile. "Apparently, I can't stay away from you."

Ashley regarded him and stayed silent.

"The flowers are for you. Sorry, they're wilted. I'll blame it on the humidity." He offered her the bouquet, wrapped in paper towels. He'd stopped by the river and gathered the spray of fiery pinks, cardinal reds, and stems of gray-purple violets.

"Thank you. They're exquisite." Ashley set down her glass, then sniffed the delicate fragrance, a woodsy scent mingling with a hint of fresh strawberries. "David, you remembered."

A declaration, not a question.

He grinned down at her. "I listened to every word you said yesterday."

"I didn't think you heard me. You were preoccupied."

"My work requires me to stay focused. Fortunately, men can do two things at once."

She lifted a skeptical eyebrow. "Can they?"

"Yes. I can listen and work at the same time."

"Really?" She planted a hand on her hip. "What else did I say yesterday?"

"Before or after you climbed the tree?"

"After."

"Well, you enlightened me on every dog breed on the globe and provided next month's weather forecast." He flicked a glance toward the window to emphasize his point. The dark-green leaves of a majestic oak tree bent in the steamy evening breeze. "And your favorite television show is the old *Andy Griffith Show*."

"Because it's the funniest sitcom ever produced," she informed him. "I laugh each time I watch an episode, even though I memorized the lines and know the outcome by heart."

"I prefer to watch documentaries on my computer."

She slanted him a cheeky glance. "Anything special?"

"*Gladiator*."

"That movie is not a documentary or entirely accurate, though it's certainly wonderful. I'd categorize it as a love story."

Slightly mollified because she hadn't disputed his taste in documentaries, he replied, "The movie is inspired by factual events in ancient Rome."

"Uh-huh. Whatever you say. You never told me your favorite show."

"I don't own a television set."

"No way." She peered at a nearby wall, where a wide-screen TV was mounted. "I've never known anyone who doesn't own a TV."

"Now you do."

She met his gaze with disbelief. "Are you some type of minimalist?"

"On the contrary, I love TV." He offered a guilty shrug. "I discovered, though, that it's too distracting and robbed me of my most valuable asset."

"Which is?"

"My time when I could be painting."

"You're here." Her sigh was edgy, as if she was blaming

herself for his presence at the inn. "You could be painting now."

He felt it—a curious tug on his heart, the odd ache whenever he reflected on how she always considered others before herself.

"Time is valuable. People are valuable." He brushed his fingers across her cheek. "Spending time with valuable people is most valuable."

She swallowed. "A lot of valuables in your sentences."

"A lot of meaning too." He smiled into her gorgeous eyes. "May I tell you the truth about something?"

"Always."

"I fantasized about kissing you. Your skin is soft, and your mouth... I'm saying words out loud I've never told another woman."

He stepped closer. Their breaths mingled.

No. He was saying too much. He thought about pulling back. He didn't.

She gazed up at him, her chin tipping ever slightly. "I'm flattered." Her voice vibrated with the same emotion.

He understood.

He kissed her, a gentle brush of his lips on hers. Sparks of adrenaline in his veins didn't match the tenderness of their kiss, he thought.

And then he stopped thinking at all.

That is, until she stepped back and firmly shook her head.

She set the flowers down, her hands flitting like a wild bird. She didn't seem to know where to put them. "You're quite thoughtful for a guy who accomplishes two tasks at once." Her tone was easy, but her mannerisms indicated otherwise. She was shaken, as he was, by their attraction.

He dragged in a long breath. "I owe you an apology."

"For what?"

"Yesterday I wasn't as attentive as I should've been."

"No apology is necessary. You're more observant than I imagined." She picked up her tea and sipped. Her hand was trembling. She glanced at him, apparently wondering if he noticed. He did.

"You're an exceptional artist, David, and need your space." She set down the glass. "I respect you for those traits. Praise God for giving you a unique talent to share with the world."

It wasn't her affirming statements that brought a swift beat to his heart. It was the manner in which she regarded him—with appreciation in her magnificent eyes and subdued marvel in her tone. It was refreshing to be viewed as a man with merit, as if he were heroic and exceptional. A gift more precious than any he'd ever received.

He debated about reaching for her again, more insistently, by circling his arms around her and keeping her close. He wanted to create a magical evening for them—to cancel out his rudeness from the prior day. He wanted to begin the night with kiss after kiss.

Upon gauging her guarded reaction, however, he instructed himself to slow down.

"Are you ready for even more truth?" he asked.

His question elicited a puzzled gaze from her, and she shuffled her feet. "Truth is always welcome, David."

"There is another important reason why I'm here tonight."

She tilted her head, searched his face. "I'm listening."

"I wanted to see you again." He fought down more words, the knowledge of spending enchanting hours with her. Truth was, he *had* to see her again.

A rosy blush crept up her cheeks. "Oh."

Not exactly the response he'd hoped for, but considering their growing relationship, he'd accept it. He assessed her rigid bearing, and his stomach plummeted. He could almost hear her refusal.

He hesitated. "Will you join me for dinner?"

Her mouth lifted at the corners. "I'd love to. Otherwise, I planned on dining alone."

He blew out a relieved breath. "Did you bring any props?"

"You're referring to *The Lonely Planet* guidebook?" She laughed. "Not tonight."

"Excellent. No distractions." *Except him.* "Let's create a celebratory occasion."

Years before, he'd read an entire book about celebrations. A modern-day spirituality book, advising the reader to rejoice in every activity. He'd never done that, embracing precious happiness as it came, and he intended to begin with Ashley.

"By ordering champagne with dinner?" She nodded over her shoulder toward the hallway.

"I don't drink alcohol. You?"

"Me neither. I prefer any beverage with sugar."

"Wow," he noted with a straight face. "You could've fooled me."

Her infectious smile was his reward for following through with his plan. He hadn't been certain she'd be willing to dine with him. He'd taken a gamble, entering the lobby with a bedraggled bouquet and a whisper in his gut that honest joy might be waiting for him around the corner.

And here it was. And here she was.

His mind flashed back to several signs he'd seen on his drive into town.

There'd been one advertising the farmer's market, another for a church bake sale, and a third for a Renaissance Faire in a nearby town.

The farmer's market was a possibility.

The Renaissance Faire? He'd never attended one, although the brochures he'd seen had always seemed to

81

suggest a gigantic costume party. He wouldn't be caught dead in one of those getups people spent months creating.

As for the church bake sale, he hadn't seen the inside of a church in years. He tried to be a good person but harbored too much pain and resentment to pray.

Realizing his presence at the inn might produce a stir of local gossip, he'd parked his pickup truck a half block away and walked to the inn. Not that it made a difference, though perhaps he might slide inside discreetly, wildflower bouquet in hand.

No such luck.

The setting sun cast long shadows on the ground as he approached. Julian greeted him with a hearty hello and a boisterous chuckle.

"I messed up when I was with Ashley yesterday," David began.

"Welcome to the human race." Julian clapped David on the back and ushered him through the hallway. "We all have our faults."

"Some more numerous than others. I'm here to ask her to dinner."

"No objections on my end, and there's nothing like an apology to set things right. I assumed you weren't hankering to dine with me tonight." With a good-natured grin, Julian continued. "Ashley is a unique, giving person. I gathered from a recent chat she highly rates your art."

David scanned the dining room, his gaze landing on his painting. "I debated calling her, but I didn't have her phone number."

"Ask her for it."

"I plan to."

"Go with your gut." Julian attended to a tray of drinks on the sideboard. "Do what's appropriate, for the finest of reasons, and you'll receive your reward."

David looked from the painting to Julian. "Is this some form of religious teaching found in the Bible?"

Julian's smirk was reassuring. "Common sense straight from yours truly."

"Then what is my reward?"

"The hazel-eyed blond sitting alone in the lounge. I'll get her for you." Julian lifted a hand in salute. "You'll learn I have a penchant for meddling in people's lives, especially when they've taken the first step and brought flowers."

With that, Julian had steered David into the parlor.

David watched Ashley now, knowing he couldn't explain, even to himself, how he felt about her. He didn't intend to examine the countless emotions compelling him to spend every minute around her. A spot-on Christian might proclaim it was God.

Maybe God. Maybe.

"David, are you coming?" Ashley had gathered the wildflowers and started for the hallway. She darted a glance over her shoulder. "I'll ask the hostess for a vase and we can leave the flowers here."

He caught up with her in two strides. "Why don't you bring the flowers into the dining room? Julian will wave his hand and a vase will magically appear."

She offered a plucky grin. "You're probably right."

"You've met Julian. I'm not *probably* right. I'm *definitely* right."

His assertion was rewarded by her bubbling laugh. Without taking his gaze from hers, he asked, "Do we need reservations for dinner?"

"Nope. I know the owner."

As they entered the hallway, he took her hand in his. "Me too."

He was heartened by the fact she didn't pull away. If anything, she nodded her acceptance.

CHAPTER 7

Action is the foundational key to all success.
- Picasso

he Cherish Hills Inn dining room lived up to the accolades David had heard about since his arrival. The walls were salmon-colored, the decorations lush gray, and tiny tea light candles on each table created an inviting ambiance to the elegant, understated atmosphere. Here, subtlety was the key. The artist in David noted these details as well as the table settings—gleaming silverware, sparkling glasses, tapered candles, and gold-rimmed china plateware. He also noted that heads swiveled, and the noise level dropped as he and Ashley walked in.

Ashley handed the flowers to the maître d', who then pulled out a chair and seated her. He assured her the flowers would be sent to her room, a complementary crystal vase provided.

"Perhaps a table closer to the window?" David asked, gesturing toward a particular table.

"Sorry, sir. The town sheriff and his wife sit there." The maître d' wore an apologetic smile as earnestly as he wore his black tuxedo.

Ashley and David scanned the menus, both opting for the signature dish of smoked ham, scalloped potatoes, and green beans topped with almonds.

After they placed their orders, including a carafe of fresh-squeezed limeade and Cobb salads for starters, David gazed at her across the table.

He couldn't get enough of her delightful, heart-shaped face. "Thank you for allowing me to be your dinner companion this evening."

"I never would have refused you." The soft warmth in her eyes and the catch in her lilting tone gave him pause. Absorbed by the feelings expanding inside him, he slid his hand across the table and rested it on hers. In the background, the piped-in harmony of a solo saxophone and bass violin added to the emotional mood.

When their salads were served, she bent her head and whispered a blessing for their food. Although he hadn't prayed in years, David reverently bowed his head. He didn't participate, though he remembered the simple prayer of grace.

When she finished her prayer, she sampled a portion of hard-boiled egg and avocado doused in vinaigrette.

"I've never tasted savory greens." She pinched two fingers together and touched her lips. "In fact, I don't usually like greens."

He agreed the salad was incredible and attributed the delectable taste to the olive-oil-based dressing and bits of bacon. He wasn't a leafy vegetable person, but figured he'd better start getting used to it, given a garden was a part of his future.

His gaze skimmed the room, and fragments of conversation swirled around him. "I'm glad I changed out of my paint-spattered clothes and decided on dress pants and a cotton button-down shirt."

"And sport coat," she reminded.

He'd draped his navy-blue sport coat over the back of his chair.

"This is a fancy place. And well-trained staff."

Their server, wearing the inn's trademark red apron, magically appeared when they were ready to order, brought their food and kept their glasses filled. Otherwise, he was satisfyingly absent.

After they savored a superb dinner and their table was cleared, David became keenly aware they were being watched by the staff.

While their server crumbed the tablecloth and replaced the silverware and water glasses, another waiter brought a fresh carafe of limeade and refilled their glasses. As before, Ashley added more sugar to hers. A cheese plate assortment with bread, crackers, and candied nuts also appeared.

Julian joined them and asked if the meal was prepared to their liking. They assured him the food was exquisite.

"Will you be having coffee or dessert?" Julian inquired. "Our featured special is blackberry sorbet." He snagged a silver water pitcher from a side table and refilled their glasses. "Our desserts are made in-house. The sorbet is refreshing, and the blackberries are local."

"We hoped you served cookies." David smiled at Ashley, noting the laughter in her eyes. "Particularly chocolate cookies."

"I'm certain our pastry chef can create something

extraordinary." Julian snatched a menu from an empty table and flipped to the dessert listings.

"Particularly frozen chocolate cookies." David smeared spicy mustard on a cracker and popped it into his mouth.

If Julian was caught off guard, he didn't show it, except for a widening of his eyes. In the meantime, Ashley's cheeks colored a hot pink.

"Excellent choice." Julian glanced toward the doorway. "I apologize for intruding on your evening, Mr. Fodero, but my wife, Nora, and our daughter, Samantha, are hoping to meet you. Samantha is attending college and keen on her course work."

"What is she studying?"

"Baroque composers—Bach, Handel and Scarlatti."

"The arts, along with novel ideas and challenges, will help her discover where her passion truly lies." David paused. "By the way, Julian, you've called me David ever since we met."

"Of course." Julian said, as though the opposite was true. "In a more formal setting, though, everything is more ... formal."

"Please ask them to come over." He had no intention of leaving Ashley out of the conversation and gestured to her. "I'm assuming they haven't met Ashley yet, either."

"I met your daughter already." Ashley scooped a handful of candied nuts.

"And I told both my wife and daughter a little more about Ashley." Julian regarded them with a warm smile.

A short while later, a dark-haired woman and a young lady, who looked to be in her early twenties, hurried to their table.

Julian quickly made the introductions while Ashley and Samantha said hello to each other.

"It's great to meet you, Mr. Fodero," Samantha said. She

looped a strand of inky-black hair behind her ear, and David couldn't help but grin at her ear piercings—three in each ear, chunky gold hoops interspersed with miniature crescent moons and stars. The young woman definitely expressed her unique style.

"David," he corrected. He kept his expression pleasant, but her exuberance discomfited him. He didn't deserve it. "Ashley merits the genuine praise. She owns an art studio and gives back to the community by providing classes to handicapped children and adults. Me? I just paint."

"I adore my profession." Ashley looked at the others, then met his approving stare. "Though you are the true artist."

"In the artist-fan relationship, both the artist and admirer are important," Julian put in. "Also, a painter works at his or her own pace. The admirer is a supporter, encourager, and exhibits patience."

Ashley murmured an agreement.

"See why my dad is so smart?" Samantha grinned and turned to Ashley. "I never used to volunteer, but after my parents coaxed me into giving it a try, I discovered that volunteering is fulfilling."

"I'm liking your parents more and more for the values they're instilling in you." David lifted his glass. "What are you studying?"

"Music is my first love." Samantha continued gawking at David whenever she looked his way. "But as much as I loved the Baroque period, I'm also studying avant-garde art, which is much more modern."

"Hurray for avant-garde." He followed her gaze and realized she was staring at his painting. "I commend you. Follow your dream."

"Her major instrument is guitar," Nora said, automatically straightening the cutlery on the table next to theirs.

"What type of music is your favorite?" David asked Samantha. Considering her age, he assumed her interests were countless. "I like all kinds of music, and especially country."

"Worship music is my choice," Julian, Nora, and Samantha announced in unison.

His gaze encompassed all three of them. Yup. He was definitely surrounded by a community that valued God and family. He studied Ashley, this gorgeous woman sitting across from him. He had tasted her mouth and sensed her pleasure in their embrace. More and more, he felt an attraction he couldn't rationalize with a flippant dismissal.

"Worship music is elevating." Ashley surveyed the cheese plate and selected a firm cheese and a slice of bread. "Whenever I listen, I feel calm. The lyrics are soothing and inspirational."

Soothing and inspirational. Like her.

David struggled to arrange his thoughts in order and discovered he already had. With her, he was at peace because she had become his inspiration.

In truth, God had once been his inspiration—to create, to bring out his level best. To enlighten him.

Sure, on occasion, particularly when the going got rough, David considered revisiting prayer. However, he always talked himself out of it, which was easy. He hadn't realized all were excuses until he'd examined his motives.

Which were?

Making justifications for things he didn't want to do. For anything that made him uncomfortable.

Like God?

He presumed God didn't wish to hear from him only during the rough patches. But perhaps there was a chance to reconnect with God. Perhaps Ashley could help him.

Ashley.

He couldn't ignore the gentle tug on his heart whenever he gazed at her. Change was happening, however subtle. With God. With Ashley.

"When are you going to start painting again, Mr. Fodero?" Samantha asked.

"Hmm?" Absorbed in reflection, he'd drifted away from the exchange.

Ashley shot him a rueful look. "He's a typical artist. Sometimes I've lost him in the middle of a discussion too."

He reached out and squeezed her hand. "In the days since we've met, Ashley is beginning to know me well."

"Uh-huh, Mr. Planter of Gardens." She plunked another sugar cube into her limeade and stirred. She did that a lot. Whenever she was uncomfortable, she craved sugar.

"Samantha," Nora said, "what a rude question." She rested a firm hand on her daughter's shoulder. "The decision is up to Mr. Fodero to decide when to paint, not you. Dad just mentioned how a fan should be patient and respect the artist."

"But the public is waiting." Undeterred, Samantha looked again at David's painting, then back at him. "More important, the entire world is waiting."

"To everything there is a season." Julian quoted the familiar Bible passage and smiled. "C'mon ladies, there's work to be done here."

"Dad, I can't help at the inn tonight." Samantha splayed her hands on her slim hips. "I have to get home and take the dog out."

"Our house is two blocks away, and the dog can wait another half hour," Nora replied, and they all chuckled at Samantha's audible groan.

"You own a dog?" David inquired.

"A golden retriever." Samantha's smile was unrestrained.

It was amazing how quickly a young person's mood shifted. "Canine Helpers is where Dad and I volunteer and it's awesome."

David nodded. "I agree. The place is awesome."

"Do you like dogs, Mr. Fodero?"

"I love dogs. In fact, I own a dachshund named Pickle." He pulled out his phone to show her a photo, then decided to go a step further. "I invested in a doggie camera so I can see Pickle when I'm not home. The camera streams to my phone."

"Pickle is adorable." Ashley favored another scoop of nuts. "Although I can't speak from experience because I don't own a pet, unless my goldfish, Frederick, counts. Fortunately, one of my friends is feeding him while I'm away. My apartment is tiny and—"

"No excuses," David countered.

The mood of pleasantness faltered, and he searched for a way to restore it.

"I'm sorry," he said. "I shouldn't judge."

Ashley frowned. "No, you shouldn't."

"Alrighty then," Julian said. "Now that we've discussed dogs and college and the arts, let's allow David and Ashley the opportunity to get better acquainted, shall we?" He smiled at them. "Your server will bring you cookies and coffee." With an apologetic grin, Julian piloted his wife and daughter from the dining room.

"Is that what we're doing?" Ashley peered at David over her glass. "Getting to know each other better? Do tell."

"First, I'm abandoning the subject of dog ownership, so you'll stop scowling at me."

She coiled a strand of silky hair around her finger and displayed a sunny smile.

"Much better." David leaned back as their waiter returned. With a flourish, the waiter poured piping-hot

91

coffee into their cups, then positioned a crystal creamer, sugar bowl, and a glass-topped plate of fancy-looking chocolate cookies in the center of the table.

Ashley went for the sugar.

David quirked an eyebrow. "Well, my beautiful companion, shall we begin?"

CHAPTER 8

Everything you can imagine is real.
–Picasso

"You first." Ashley used a silver tong to pick up three sugar cubes and plunked them into her coffee. "How about a story from your childhood, David?"

"Anything in particular?"

"How many siblings do you have?"

He eyed her coffee, frothing with sugar. "Two older brothers and a younger sister. I'm a middle child. There was lots of boisterous shouting over the din of flag football tournaments on our front lawn or when fixing cars in our garage."

"You're mechanical?"

"Not even a little. My brothers are excellent mechanics, though."

93

"Are you athletic?" She gave him the once-over, her gaze lingering on his shoulders.

"I jog and I've got a workout room in my condo in New York. Plus, I played football in high school." He blew out a breath. "Mostly to please my father, who was intent on raising his sons to be jocks. He was a competitive sportsman and almost made it to the pros."

"Were you a jock?"

"Football earned me dates with girls who would never have looked at me otherwise." David laughed. "I concentrated on painting and artwork. Perusing art galleries and sketching were my favorite Saturday afternoon pastimes."

"Tell me more."

His jaw tensed, and he forced himself to relax.

He expected the interest—the "getting to know each other" conversation Julian had endorsed. He just wasn't used to opening up to people. "My father wanted his sons to live up to his legacy as a star athlete."

Ashley provided an unabashed smile. "You're a star painter."

"Believe me, it's not the same." He pushed back his coffee cup.

"Instead, you lived up to the art world's expectations and well beyond."

His nod was quick, though he fell silent. The waiter came by, refilled their coffee cups and pointedly looked at the untouched cookie plate.

"I promise we'll eat all the cookies." Ashley smiled at the waiter, who quickly disappeared, then shifted her gaze to David. "You accomplished your numerous successes in your own style."

Evidently sensitive to his moods and body language, she had realized the significance of their conversation and how much his father's opinion mattered to him. Even now, after all these years. Even now, after all the rotten things his father had done.

He lifted the glass top off the plate and offered her a cookie. "Delicious, fancy chocolate."

She chuckled. "Excellent subject change."

"I try."

"I prefer plain store-bought cookies with a creamy center."

"Are you easy to please?"

"Sometimes."

"You're hedging."

"So are you." She laughed, then bit into the cookie. "These aren't frozen and taste more like fudge."

"They're posher and more expensive."

Thoughtfully, she chewed. "As long as I'm scarfing down chocolate, I'm happy. Any food from the inn's kitchen is awesome."

His mood relaxed, and their banter once again became upbeat.

The flickering candlelight cast a gleam on her thick blond hair, transforming it to silver. Her creamy complexion glowed.

She glided her fingers around the rim of her limeade glass. Her hands were slim and graceful, her fingernails cut short and tapered. She was a natural beauty.

The cozy, romantic atmosphere, along with the melodic background violins, enhanced her loveliness and brought a sparkle to the entire evening.

He wanted her to describe her art students. He enjoyed how her face lit up whenever she mentioned them. When he was about to shift the conversation toward her, she asked, "Do you see your father often?"

"No. He passed away."

"Oh. I'm sorry."

95

"Thanks."

"Well." She cleared her throat. "Did you used to see your father often?"

"No."

"That was an abrupt answer."

"He was a difficult guy. Like father, like son, I've been told." David sighed. "When I attended elementary school, I learned he was unfaithful to my mother."

"How did you find out?"

"He and a woman I didn't know brought me to a circus. I was confused because the woman wasn't my mother. He made me promise never to tell anyone."

"Did you?"

"I was seven." The memory of his father's stern lectures still resounded in David's brain. "You want the short answer? No. He died over a decade ago and his secret died with him."

"Did you ever wish to snatch back your promise and tell your mother?"

"Oh, I considered it many times. My heart broke for her since she had a good-hearted and trusting nature. But I was a little kid and taught to obey. Invariably, I struggled to please him."

He'd never succeeded.

Ashley snatched another cookie, pulling it apart before dipping it into her coffee. "And your mother?"

"She was my biggest cheerleader."

"So, she never learned of your father's unfaithfulness?"

"If she did, she never let on. I guess she trusted him." Unlike David. He'd learned not to trust his father. He hardly trusted anybody.

Ashley folded her hands and stayed silent.

"My mother's beauty was ageless," David went on. "No plastic surgery for her, though she insisted on dyeing her hair to cover the gray."

"Was her hair brown in her youth?"

"I believe so. Her parents immigrated to the United States from Scotland, although none of her children inherited her coloring. We all favored our Italian father's Mediterranean looks."

"Thus your attractive combination of dark hair and blue eyes."

He grinned. "I'm attractive?"

Ashley swallowed. Her cheeks flushed to her ears. "A little."

"You're attractive too. The difference is, you're attractive a lot."

"Wait, a minute." She fixed him with a stare that wouldn't let go. "Is the mysterious woman in your painting *Woman by the River*, your mother?"

"Very observant." He tugged at the collar of his shirt. "Though the woman isn't mysterious when you analyze my motives."

"Which are?"

"I add whoever is special to me and my life to my paintings."

"Like your dog. Like your mother. Anyone else?"

"Nope. Often, my mother whispered words of praise in my ear. About my art," he clarified. "Every night after prayers, she'd encourage me to continue sketching and painting."

"I like to hear that."

"Hear what?"

"I like to hear about prayers and encouragement."

He shifted. "Right."

Her head crooked to the side. "You have a problem with encouragement?"

"Nope."

"Prayer?"

Despite her reproachful tone, her eyes held kind gentleness.

"Prayer ..." He paused and pondered. "Sometimes." He replied cautiously, not wishing to tread on a religious landmine, especially with a devout believer like Ashley. This was territory he hadn't navigated since his teens. "If I'm candid, I have a problem with prayer. Or rather, unanswered prayers."

"Try again. You'll find solace by talking to God."

"To each his own." He grabbed her hand. "Prayer isn't for me. If it's for you, I'm pleased you've found comfort."

"Comfort is only the beginning." She withdrew her hand. "Your mother heartily approved of your art?"

"She motivated me often whenever I wanted to quit."

He was telling Ashley more than he'd ever told anyone about his childhood, but he refused to scrutinize the emotions welling up inside him that urged him to keep speaking.

She was easy to talk to, her gaze focused solely on him.

"Please go on," she urged.

"When I was awarded a generous art scholarship to NYU, my father finally sat up and took notice, though afterward I hardly heard from him. Which is why I settled in New York City instead of moving back home."

"Where is home?"

David wrapped his hands around his cup. "A seacoast town in Georgia."

"I'm sure the area is lovely." Ashley touched his hand, her fingers lingering. Her hand seemed to gravitate back to him of its own accord. "And now?"

He didn't have an answer. Remembrances flashed of his father's final days and how David had stayed by his bedside, although his father hadn't recognized him.

Ashley opened her mouth, closed it, opened it again. "What about your brothers?"

"We don't speak. I've tried to connect, and they seldom reply. They're simply not interested. In this day and age, it's hard to believe guys think anything to do with art is a dreamer's profession reserved for sissies. I suspect they're embarrassed of me."

"You're kidding."

"I wish." He regarded the somber twist of her lips. "Happy finish, though. After undergraduate and graduate studies, New York City started to feel like home."

"Now you've landed in Cherish."

"These days, I'm living the dream."

"Which is?"

"The freedom of answering to no one."

"A confirmed bachelor?"

"Maybe."

For the time being, he added to himself.

Her mannerisms quieted. Was she interested in him, and not thrilled by his "confirmed bachelor" declaration?

No. Not possible. She was an engaging, enterprising woman who devoted her life to helping others. He was a painter who couldn't sketch a tree branch.

She picked up her fork and pressed down the cookie crumbs left on her plate. Her silence spurred him to continue.

"Both of my brothers were varsity athletes. Quinn, my sister, played soccer all through high school and college. In fact, Quinn reminds me of your friend Sarah."

"Sarah is an extremely capable woman. She hasn't allowed deafness to hamper her story. Once she recognized her disability and acknowledged she needed treatment, she embraced it. Beforehand, she waded through stages."

He leaned forward. "Such as?"

"What you might expect. Shame, refusal to accept her body's faults."

99

He gave himself fair warning. He was inquiring about Sarah and how she coped, though he was also interested in his own disability. "What's the result?"

Ashley bit down on her lower lip. "Sarah exhibits more self-confidence now. She's focused, and she recently declared life's too short not to value every hour. She's pleasant, practical, and I'm proud to call her a wonderful friend."

David pushed out a sigh he didn't realize he was holding.

Perhaps he should come to terms with his own disability instead of ignoring it and expecting it to go away. Perhaps hope beckoned. The prospect brought optimism to his heavy heart.

"My sister is an accomplished woman and well-educated," he said. "Though I don't see her much anymore."

"Why not?" Ashley offered him another cookie, which he refused.

"I only like them frozen." He shook his head. "Your tastes in food are wearing off on me."

"Try another cookie, anyway." With that, she plunked a cookie on his plate and asked again, "Why not?"

"Why not what?"

"Why aren't you in touch with your sister anymore?"

He waved an airy hand. "The artistic community is incredibly active in Manhattan, and obviously, I need a presence there because of my profession."

"Obviously."

He decided to follow Ashley's lead and dropped a sugar lump into his coffee. After stirring, he sipped and grimaced. Way ... too sweet. He set his spoon beside his napkin. "Quinn lives in Texas and is mostly married."

"Mostly?"

"She recently filed for a divorce from her current husband and tends to relocate often. She doesn't have children."

"Current husband?"

"Her third."

"Oh."

"Soon my sister will be footloose and fancy free. I love her, yet we fell out of step."

There was no better explanation. Quinn had never understood his art—had never understood *him*. She embraced traditional art, seeing no point in upside-down dogs and neon-green trees painted on the side of a building. Whenever the occasion arose, she told him as much.

"I'm sorry," Ashley whispered.

"I suppose it's my fault." He shrugged. "I tend to be cynical regarding relationships."

"Logical, considering your father's infidelity. Don't be hard on yourself and never forget how successful you are."

"Success is the part everyone remembers. However, failure defined my in-between years." He picked up the creamer. Perhaps his coffee needed cream to offset the sugary taste. "Enough about me. What about you?"

"My upbringing was the opposite of yours. Nothing rowdy. Mine was quiet because my household consisted of me and a parent."

He filled his cup to the brim with cream and tried it. Grimacing again, he decided black coffee was much better than the other options. "Your mother raised you?"

"My father. From when I was a toddler, he taught me all God's creatures are my friend."

"Where is he now?"

"Sadly, he died five years ago, and I never knew my mother. She abandoned us when I was a newborn. Years later, I learned she'd died in a car accident a few states away. She'd been speeding late at night and drinking heavily."

David kept his attention fixed on her. "She was an alcoholic?"

Ashley bobbed a yes.

"Why did you open an art studio for children with disabilities?"

"I had trouble reading when I was young. I assumed all the letters were supposed to be backward." Ashley ran a hand through her hair. "Turns out, they weren't."

"Did you attend college?"

"I attended a state school where I was a dual art education and disability studies major. I was a shy kid, and daydreaming became a favorite pastime. I always wanted to teach art to children with special needs, and thus my two passions merged."

David nodded. "And you're single."

"I'm thirty and definitely single."

"Then I shouldn't be looking over my shoulder for an irate boyfriend?"

"Hardly. I dated a guy for a couple years."

"What happened?"

"He dumped me."

Their gazes met. David refused to let go. "The guy is a fool."

Her cheeks colored. She looked away, focusing on the tiny pinpricks of candlelight flickering from each table.

They lingered over coffee, neither one willing to break the spell of attraction that drew them closer. David didn't want the night to end. He sensed she felt the same.

An hour later, in the nearly deserted dining room, their laughter still rang out. The waitstaff unobtrusively glanced at them and smiled as they cleared the other tables.

David peered at his watch. Nearly ten o'clock, and the restaurant was scheduled to close.

"Thank you, Ashley." He sought to remove himself from the magnetic spell they'd created by capping their evening with politeness. "Again, I apologize."

"You apologized already for not listening to me yesterday."

"Indeed, we established I *was* listening."

She propped her chin on her palms. "You thanked me for the peaches."

"Then thank you for the past few hours. Too few." His voice was hoarse, and he scarcely recognized it as his own. "After you left ..."

Her eyebrows shot to her hairline. "You're referring to when I stormed off?"

"Yes." He laughed out loud. It felt freeing to laugh. "I like your honesty." He liked a lot more than that about her. He liked everything.

He fished in the pocket of his sport jacket. "May I show you a photograph I took?"

"The one of the tree?"

"And you."

She sat back. "Me?"

"You happened to be in several photos."

"*Happened*? How?"

"I didn't realize it." Or maybe he did. In any case, he'd blamed the mistake on his failing eyesight.

He slid the photo across the table. The tree and flowers were clear. However, Ashley, clad in shorts and a chambray top and sitting in the tree, took center focus. "I'd welcome your permission to paint you."

"Why?"

His gaze was steady. "Because you're beautiful."

"David, I'm definitely not—"

He pressed a finger to her lips, stopping her from protesting. "You really don't realize it? Your humbleness is disarming."

"Reality, you mean." Appreciation edged her self-conscious laughter. "But thank you."

He felt as if a warm hand had settled on his heart. This woman unearthed sentiments he'd buried long ago, bringing him a newfound excitement and pleasure. She was unpretentious, yet joyful. Kind and truthful.

Inwardly, his conscience chided him. A permanent relationship between them wasn't practical. Besides the fact she lived miles away, she was a people person.

Him? He preferred to sit back and observe the world.

Nonetheless, he captured her fingers. "Is that a yes? I can paint you?"

"You have my permission, but only if I can see the painting."

"After it's done, and not before."

That's it. Establish a practical boundary. Finish the evening with a kiss on her cheek and a "'Have a good life. I'll call you.'"

He did the opposite.

He came around the table to pull out her chair, then inched closer.

He scanned the dining room. Empty. Julian and the wait staff had disappeared. When had that happened? He had been so engrossed in everything about Ashley, he hadn't paid attention to his surroundings. Even the violins had been shut off.

He tipped up her chin. "How long will you be in Cherish?"

"I intend to travel back to my studio somewhat soon, because I miss my students. Thankfully, a couple volunteer instructors are filling in for me." Her gaze drifted to his. "Initially, I arranged to be here only for the weekend."

"You're extending your stay because…?"

"I like it here."

"I like it here too." He dipped his head and brushed his lips against hers in a tender kiss. "Especially because you're in town."

"Church service on Sunday was wonderful."

"An invitation?"

"Definitely."

"Church." He sighed. "I'll paint the outside. No reason for me to venture inside. Let's leave it at that."

Her fingers teased the soft hairs at his nape. "Perhaps—"

His arms wrapped around her, and he captured the rest of her words in a long kiss.

"Dining room is officially closed, folks." Julian's deep voice came from the doorway. "You can continue smooching in the hall." He flipped the light switch, and the room sank into darkness. "Our generous Lord will give each of us another day."

A minute later, Ashley and David reached the lobby, hand in hand.

"I'll settle up for tonight's meals," David said to a waiting Julian.

Julian winked. "I'm certain you'll be back and will keep a tab running."

"I'll walk you to the door." Ashley linked arms with David and led the way to the front entrance.

"Thanks." He grinned. "What are your plans for tomorrow?"

"I want to revisit Aaron's art shop."

"Aaron is a nice guy."

"Yes." Her tone was soft, her smile warm.

David pieced together her missing words. She hadn't extended her reservation in Cherish to purchase art supplies. She was staying in town because of him. He knew this as surely as his heart took a beat.

The upcoming days held infinite appeal, though his mind shouted a reminder. What could come of a serious relationship? Three months had always been his dating limit.

Luckily, it hadn't been three months yet.

And afterward? Was a long-distance relationship with Ashley possible?

He rubbed a hand over his chin.

In fairness to Ashley, he needed to attend to his vision problem first. There was no quick fix, and although his brain had adjusted, the disability was affecting his painting. He couldn't even paint a tree.

His art, his vision, his problem.

All well and good, although he clung to a decision he couldn't believe, considering there was no future with Ashley. Still, the idea took shape without warning.

"How about a tour of the town's main attraction tomorrow?" he asked.

"What is the main attraction?"

"A surprise."

Her hazel eyes widened. "You're still a newcomer here."

"Compared to your mere days, I'm a lifelong resident." He hesitated. "May I have your cellphone number?"

"Phone the reception desk and they'll transfer your call to my room."

"I'd prefer to text you directly."

One eyebrow cocked. "We hardly know each other."

"In case you haven't figured it out, I'm trying to change that."

She drew her cell phone from her purse and handed it to him. He texted himself and checked his phone. Then he texted her back. *Will you accompany me tomorrow?*

He handed the phone to her.

With a grin reaching her eyes, she replied, *Where?*

He pulled her into his arms, more than delighted she rewarded his kiss with gratifying acceptance. "A surprise, remember? I'll text you in the morning. I have somewhere special in mind."

For tomorrow. And the next day. And the day after that.

CHAPTER 9

It takes a long time to become young.
– Picasso

t daybreak, Ashley woke in her luxurious room at the inn. She drew back the snowy-white lace curtains framing the window and peered outside. The morning streets were quiet, and the whiff of buttery, yeasty biscuits from the kitchen wafted through the air. The sky was bathed in the rosy radiance of sunrise.

She debated about working out and rationalized that walking and hiking with David sufficed.

Excuses, excuses.

The bouquet of wildflowers the maître d' had sent to her room, vibrant and cheerful, held center stage in a gleaming crystal vase on a side table. She envisioned David revisiting the river, bending to choose the exact flowers she'd favored. He was a man capable of thoughtfulness and tenderness, and no one could fault her for being helplessly drawn to him.

She resolved to keep her wits about her. Attraction was fleeting. Promises of a commitment called for something else entirely. Honesty, integrity, and a long-lasting love.

As the morning hours passed and she waited for David's text, she felt increasingly guilty.

She'd sought him out over false pretenses, and it was wrong. She was a Christian woman. How could she explain to him that her car breaking down in front of his cabin hadn't been a coincidence?

She opened the pocket Bible she'd brought with her. Her father had taught her to study the verses and pray often. Today she began with Romans 8:31 and reflected on the message.

If God was for her, who could be against her? God's presence in her life didn't mean she'd never face sorrow. Instead, the words held the promise she'd never experience sorrow alone, for He was always with her.

"Dear Lord," she whispered. "Allow faith to remain my focus. I must do better. I can count on God. Can He count on me?"

Assuredly, she made excuses and there were things she should have done differently, but she vowed to learn from her missteps and apply them to her upcoming decisions. Today she had wisdom. Today she would tell David the truth of why she was in Cherish before courage abandoned her. A relationship depended on her coming clean with him.

He had trust issues and valued honesty. Had he truly believed she'd gotten lost on a one-way street in the middle of nowhere?

Don't shift the blame onto his shoulders, she scolded herself. This was all her doing. He had no reason not to accept her explanation when she'd landed on his doorstep, which only made matters worse.

In times of conflict, she prayed. She did so now in a

hushed whisper, without reservation. "Lord, in the midst of my uncertainty, I praise your glory and honor. I value your consistent presence in my life. Please do not give up on me. I appreciate that you are ever faithful."

David's text appeared on her phone screen just as a pleasant young waitress arrived with a continental breakfast tray. After Ashley positioned the tray on a table by the window, she clicked on the text.

Good morning, gorgeous, David began.

Top of the morning to you too.

Did you sleep well?

His question unsettled her, because all her dreams had been of him. She grasped the china coffeepot and poured steaming coffee into her cup.

Ashley?

I'm here. Yes, I slept well. You?

I painted until midnight. I was inspired. Pickle stayed up and kept me company.

Against her better judgment, she asked, *What did you paint?*

He didn't reply, but somehow, she already knew. He'd been painting her. As the image took hold, she hoped he hadn't sketched her with unruly blond hair and her cowlick sticking straight up. And what about her pointed chin?

Worse, had he attached her nose to her face? One never could be certain with avant-garde artists.

I kept wondering if you enjoyed yourself last night.

She reread his text. Now why would he wonder about that? His question sounded insecure, yet David was strong and confident. She could see it in his artwork, his paintings bold and emotional.

She nodded at the phone, then felt foolish because he couldn't see her. *I enjoyed myself very much. It was fun.*

It was magical, she thought.

I still feel your hand in mine.

Her heart quickened at his message. Had he really typed something that romantic?

I'll pick you up at eleven.

She paused in the act of stirring three sugar lumps into her coffee and typed, *Where are we going?*

We might go on a hike.

Might?

I'll pack everything we need.

Food?

Are cookies okay? Just kidding. He inserted a smiley emoji. *Wear comfortable shoes.*

TWO HOURS LATER, she waited in the inn's sunny, plant-filled lobby. She'd decided on lightweight jeans, a long-sleeved blouse, cotton socks, and serviceable hiking boots. She didn't intend to get bit up by mosquitoes. Also, she carried a tan leather tote bag.

A foray into her suitcase had yielded the boots she'd brought on a whim, and she was thankful. Surely God had a hand in this.

The inn provided miniature bottles of lemon and sage soap and shampoo, and the scent was heavenly. The discovery had delighted her. She was one of those women who dashed to the hotel bathroom first to check out the toiletries.

After her shower, she'd wrapped herself in a luxurious, blue-striped terry robe and applied a touch of blush and a rosy lip gloss.

She'd secured her freshly washed hair into a ponytail, then loaded her tote bag with essentials—sunscreen, a water bottle, and a thin cotton sweater in case the weather got cool.

Unlikely, though. Sunshine poured in the front window, the blue sky speckled with clouds, and the weatherman predicted ninety-degree temperatures and the prerequisite humidity.

Julian strode over, displaying a smirk she could only describe as amused. "Greetings, Ashley. Are you sticking around for anyone in particular?"

"David suggested we see a little of Cherish today."

Julian wiped minuscule dust particles off the bannister with his fingers. "What a thoughtful guy. I give a fellow credit when he seizes a golden opportunity and runs with it."

She raised her chin. "He's showing me around because he's been in Cherish longer."

"A whole few months longer. Though it's a superb excuse for a date."

"This isn't a date."

"If you say so." He chuckled. "Where are you two exploring?"

"He mentioned a hike."

"Probably Juniper Mountain, the town's favorite."

"Sarah spoke about the Walnut Forest route. She claims the climb is easy." Ashley shoved her hair from her forehead. "I'll point that fact out to David."

"Don't forget bug spray."

"He's packing everything."

Julian laughed. "I applaud a guy who thinks ahead."

Before Ashley responded, David entered the lobby, clad in jean shorts and a gray T-shirt, and cradling Pickle under one arm. She considered that his tanned, strong-featured face belonged on the big screen of a Hollywood movie. Yet he preferred to live as a hermit and paint.

"I trust you don't mind I brought Pickle," David announced to Julian. "As you can see, I'm holding him."

"I do." Julian nodded. "As a reminder, Frank's Pizza allows dogs."

"Thanks for the tip."

Julian extended his hand to David and exchanged a friendly shake. "And I recognize Pickle from your painting that hangs in our dining room."

"You're very discerning."

"I try."

"Good morning, Ashley." David's admiring gaze fixed on her, moving gradually down her face, hair, and legs. He bent his head and their lips touched. "You are exquisite, as always."

His words caused her stomach to flutter with anticipation, and his fleeting kiss ignited a spark she hadn't felt in years. "You're not too shabby yourself."

A smile crept across his face. "And your hair smells like—"

"Lemons," she and Julian chorused.

Julian brightened. "The inn sourced our toiletries to a local woman who makes her own garden-inspired soaps and shampoos. She's experimenting with a variety of different perfumes."

"Tell her to stick with lemons," David replied.

Ashley patted the bag hoisted on her shoulders. "I'm ready for our surprise."

"Some surprise." He dropped his gaze to her hiking boots, muttering an effective analysis for their mutual foolishness to hike on such a hot day.

She burst out laughing. "We live in the South. Get used to scorching summer weather."

He joined in with a chuckle. Reaching for her hand, he led her to the front door.

"Bye, you two," Julian called out. "I'm clearly invisible because you only have eyes for, well, you two. Oh, and by the way, Tom, the previous owner of the inn, didn't allow dogs inside."

Ashley peeked over her shoulder. "We appreciate your flexibility, Julian."

He beamed. "Who am I to enforce the rules? I'm just the owner."

DAVID PROVED A PROPER GENTLEMAN, exhibiting old-world manners. He insisted on opening the passenger door of his truck for her before dashing to the driver's side and buckling Pickle into a dog harness in the seat behind her. The truck's interior smelled of oil and canvas and paint. She recognized the scents from her art studio and recalled the same smells when she'd entered David's cabin.

After they buckled their seat belts, he switched on the radio, and while Tim McGraw sang, she stole a glance at David. He sat on the ripped leather seat beside her and stared straight ahead. She sensed his need to focus and surmised it was because of his failing eyesight.

He glanced sideways at her. "Before our hike, there are a couple places I'd like to show you."

"You're the tour guide and the driver. Will we stop at Aaron's Art Shop?"

"Let's save the art excursion for another day."

Another day. Her heart squeezed. Another day to spend with this compelling man.

Despite any misgivings, happiness drifted through her. They were two friends savoring a scenic day together. Indeed, she envisioned herself looking back someday and reliving her hours with David as summer memories to cherish.

As they passed the sign advertising the Renaissance Faire, she sighed. "If I had more time, I'd choose to spend a day at the Faire."

"You do now."

"Do what?"

He sent her a smile. "You're staying for the week instead of a few days."

"True." She relaxed in her seat. "Have you ever gone to a Faire?"

"Never. In fact, wild horses couldn't drag me there." He paused. "Unless it meant a lot to you."

She was not only speechless, but she was also unexpectedly touched. He was considering her happiness before his own. That particular trait had been noticeably absent in her past relationships.

"First stop is Canine Helpers." He slowed his truck. "The volunteers train dogs to assist veterans."

"Samantha mentioned that she and Julian volunteer here."

"Yes. Scarlett Slater will show us around."

"Who is she?"

"A woman with a heart of gold."

Ashley sighted the sign and turnoff ahead. "You donated a painting to benefit the Canine Helpers auction."

David darted her a glance. "Close-knit communities. Nothing stays hush-hush for long, and everyone knows everybody."

At the intersection, he flicked on his turn signal.

She flashed a glance behind her. Pickle was contentedly snoring in the back seat. "Is your generosity a secret?"

"I'm delighted to help." He parked and rounded the truck to open the door for her. He woke Pickle up, unbuckling and then leashing him. He steered them to the entrance, where a woman with flaming red hair and a generous smile greeted them.

"David Fodero. Such an honor to see you again." The woman showed them inside, and David placed a hand beneath Ashley's elbow.

"Scarlett Slater, please meet Ashley Madden, my special friend."

Ashley smiled at the introduction. She and David were friends. Special friends. Whether she was being naive or idealistic, her pulse quickened with the observation.

She glanced at him, surprised to find him intently watching her.

Scarlett beamed at Ashley. "Any friend of David's is a friend of mine. His painting commanded ten thousand dollars at our silent auction, and the money will go toward supplies for the vets. We are a Christian facility and welcome donations of any amount."

Ashley digested the mind-boggling sum a patron had paid for one of David's paintings while David explained, "Owning a dog is like having a child."

"Dogs give us absolute allegiance." Scarlett crouched to rub Pickle's head, then stood. "C'mon into the common room. We've done various improvements since you were last here, David, beginning with a new sink."

As they toured the facility, Ashley asked what type of services Canine Helpers offered.

"We specially train service dogs and match them with veterans who require emotional or physical support." Scarlett gestured to a row of leashes hanging on a wall. "Many of the men and women in our armed forces return home with PTSD or physical restrictions."

David's blue eyes lit with compassion. "Canine Helpers furnishes the animals and the assistance at no charge to the veterans."

"Our aim is to ensure our veterans lead healthy, positive lives again." Scarlett spoke with such earnestness; Ashley was taken aback by the woman's commitment. "Luckily, grants and generous donors like David's contribution to our auction help the organization remain viable."

"I wish there was a way I could help too." Ashley's gaze encompassed the clean dog dishes neatly lined up.

"Some elderly folks are donating dogs they expect will be of wonderful service." Scarlett stacked retrieval toys—discs and balls and rope tugs. "Are you available to foster a dog?"

Ashley shook her head. "My apartment is tiny."

Scarlett bent to tidy a group of empty water bowls, then stood to face Ashley. "You aren't required to train the dog, if that's the reason for your reluctance."

"I don't live in Cherish. I'm visiting. At home, I work twelve-hour days." She replied as if the reasons were clear. "It's unfair for a dog to be alone all day."

"If you're ever interested at a later time when you're not as busy, here's my cell phone number." Scarlett handed Ashley a business card.

Ashley dragged her gaze from the card to David's face. His features were undecipherable, though he hadn't lectured her about dog ownership. In fact, he hadn't uttered a word.

He gave her hand a reaffirming squeeze. "You'll recognize when the time is right."

"Eventually." Ashley placed the card in her pocket. "A dog is somewhere in my future."

"Hopefully sooner rather than later." David paid for a bone baked on the premises and gave it to Pickle. The dog whined, carried the bone in his mouth, then quickly consumed it. "Sooner is better. A dog offers devoted companionship and you're missing out."

"I've elected Frederick, my goldfish, as my only pet for the time being," she replied.

A few minutes later, Ashley, Pickle and David emerged from Canine Helpers. Scarlett had recommended they visit the music store, Musically Yours, located a few blocks away.

"My darling husband, Joseph, teaches guitar lessons there." Scarlett's green eyes had radiated with affection.

"Currently, he's on a two-week tour of the eastern United States. Often, I accompany him. This time, I opted to stay in town to facilitate the training for some new dogs. However, Dorothy Edwards, the owner, will show you the music store."

"I've met her." Ashley tightened her ponytail. "I stopped in, and she told me all about Percy Grainger."

"Who is Percy Grainger?" David asked.

"He was born in Australia but is considered an American composer. Dorothy mentioned he had several peculiar obsessions."

David looked intrigued. "Spill the details."

"He gave up meat and ate mostly fruit pies."

"Better than copious amounts of sugar," he joked.

"David donated a painting to Dorothy's music shop," Scarlett said, steering the discussion back to Musically Yours. "I'm certain she'd love to see you both. I'll text her."

Agreeing, David and Ashley linked arms and exited. When all three were settled in his truck, he started the engine. There was minimal traffic on the short drive and they soon reached the corner of Myrtle and Magnolia, where the store was located.

"Scarlett's husband is a well-known contemporary worship musician." Ashley signaled to David to move closer to the curb as he parked. "I didn't put that together until you introduced her. Have you heard of Joseph Slater?"

"I don't listen to church music. Country is better."

"I disagree. Country music lyrics are all about cowboys and muddy trucks and—"

"Are you kidding? Every song tells a story. Though I recall 'worship music is your choice.'" He finger quoted with one hand, echoing the statement she, Julian, Nora, and Samantha had affirmed at dinner.

Ashley nudged his elbow. "God's grace is the best choice of all."

"Your words, not mine."

"What did you like most about church while you were growing up?"

"You don't want to hear my answer."

His confusing reply brought additional questions to mind. She sat up straighter. "Of course I do."

"To begin with, the pastor was kind."

"And the sermons?"

"I was a kid."

"Meaning you fell asleep?"

"Meaning I carried a small pad and pencil with me and sketched the pastor."

"Flattering renditions, I hope?"

"You can hope. However, on the bright side, I recall the message from one particular sermon that always stayed with me. 'The blessing ahead of you is bigger than any battle you left behind.'"

"Hallelujah, David. You had a wise pastor."

"Sometimes."

She ignored the amusement in his tone. "Go on."

"What I liked most were the refreshments served afterwards in the basement." He studied her in a beat of silence. "My mother used to bake a spicy cinnamon coffee cake with a streusel crumb topping."

"Nothing surpasses the food prepared in a church kitchen."

"Agreed. I'd sneak a cup of coffee, which was probably the beginning of my addiction to caffeine."

"You're blaming your caffeine addiction on church and your mother's coffee cake?"

Somehow, he managed to look innocent. "I told you that you wouldn't like my answer."

"Why did you stop attending?" She prayed David hadn't gotten involved in drugs or alcohol or the wrong crowd.

"Life got busy." His tone grew soft. "Life was good. I didn't need God."

The tension in the truck became smothering. She fixed him with a level stare that might have coerced a longer explanation from him had he glanced at her. However, he lowered his window and scanned the street.

A hot breeze blew inside the truck, along with the guarantee of heavy air awaiting their afternoon.

"Do you need God now?" she asked.

He met her stare, his features completely bland. "God and I don't have a running dialogue. At least, not anymore."

"One of the most profound blessings God offers is peace." She spurred herself to press onward. David harbored fears, as did everyone, but surely God would reveal Himself, allowing David to release his burdens. "He hears you," she added.

David tapped his fingers on the steering wheel. "If only He listened."

To inspire his observations, she presented a radiant smile. "You're not confident He listens, or you don't reach out to Him?"

"Both. Neither."

Silence followed his reply.

"I waited for God to communicate with me." He expelled a heavy sigh. "Nothing. Naught. Zilch. Now that I could use His guidance, He never answers."

"Why do you need His help?" She prayed David might confide to her about his vision. She wanted to comfort him, though she didn't wish to overstep her bounds.

"Because I'm human, although I like to believe I'm superhuman."

"Don't we all."

David didn't miss a beat. "I suppose you're going to lecture me on how I should pray regularly."

"I won't, then." Too tense to say more, she gazed out the passenger side at the scenic beauty of brick sidewalks, tidy shops, and window boxes overflowing with speckled petunias and dusty miller. Then she turned back to him. "Follow your heart."

"My heart is silent more often than not these days." His expression was laced with uncertainty. "Do you remember when I asked Sarah if her husband was a musician?"

"Are you changing the subject?"

"Religion is too deep a subject for such a fine summer day."

To him, maybe. Certainly not her.

Nonetheless, she'd spent enough time with David to detect his subtle nuances. Currently, his tone brought an end to their religious discourse.

"Besides," he went on. "I have something else in mind." He drew her close for a heady, unexpected kiss.

She pulled back a cautious distance. "We should go inside the store. Dorothy is expecting us."

"I'm looking forward to meeting her. Julian told me that Dorothy is a pianist, and her husband is an opera singer."

Ashley wondered if the conversation would proceed down the same path as when David compared his blindness to Beethoven's deafness.

Instead, he said, "I respect all musicians. I'm one myself."

"You are multi-talented?"

"I played the oboe in high school." He retrieved Pickle from his dog harness. "You?"

"I've never been able to sing on pitch. I took piano lessons for a couple years when I entered middle school, though I don't remember how to read a single note."

"My sister is taking piano lessons." David set Pickle on the ground and leashed the dog. "I hope Dorothy allows dogs."

"This entire community is dog-friendly."

"Another positive aspect of living in Cherish."

They lingered a half hour in the music store, chatting with Dorothy, favoring the harp earrings, and perusing stacks of sheet music.

After they left with an assortment of classical piano books for David's sister, he declared, "Now it's time for our hike."

"I don't expect you to devote your entire day to me," Ashley said as they walked hand in hand to his truck. "I'm assuming you should get back to your commissioned painting."

"I'm taking the day off."

"Are you making progress on the painting?"

A sardonic smile formed on his lips. "It's too soon to tell."

"Have you started it yet?"

"I'm waiting for inspiration to strike."

He picked up speed as they traveled on the two-lane road toward Juniper Mountain. She slanted glances at him when he wasn't looking. He had a magnificent profile, resembling a classical statue with his Roman nose and chiseled features.

During their drive, she determined he didn't have any peripheral vision to the right and could only see her if he turned his head or she sat forward. She did so, careful to make conversing as effortless as possible for him.

When they reached Juniper Mountain's parking area, he eased his truck into a space beside a vintage turquoise convertible with a "Just Married" banner draped over the rear bumper.

"How romantic." She glanced at David and was pleased he nodded in agreement. "The newlyweds must be camping to celebrate their marriage."

"Would you ever go camping on your honeymoon?"

"I'm more of a city girl." She hid her sentimentality behind a shrug. "You?"

"Whatever my future wife wanted, I'd comply without question. Her happiness would be my first priority."

"You don't seem the compliant type."

"Depends on the woman I marry. She may wind me around her little finger." He shut the ignition and covered her teasing lips with his.

Time dissolved.

The pad of his thumb smoothed her cheek. "Ashley Madden, you unbalance me," he murmured.

Her heart flipped over in her chest. His quiet utterance had a magical effect. She closed her eyes and savored his kisses. His male scent—woodsy and sandalwood—enveloped her, and she ran her fingers along his muscled forearms.

Sensing his gaze on her, she opened her eyes. She wondered what he'd say next and was surprised when he pulled back.

He blew out a breath. "Let's plan our hike for some other time."

"Why? We came all this way."

"In Cherish, everything is close. The middle of the afternoon isn't ideal for a sweltering trek up a mountain."

"What can we do instead?" Cautiously, she considered bringing up the idea of the Renaissance Faire but decided David's reaction wouldn't be positive.

His gaze rested on her lips, within inches of his. "I'll switch on the air conditioning, and we can continue kissing."

"Try another option."

He sighed. "Let's order a pizza, then enjoy a late lunch in my vintage kitchen."

"Your cabin is tastefully appointed, except for the absurd redwood chair."

"What's wrong with my chair?"

"No one in their right mind would ever sit in it."

"Why not?"

"It doesn't look at all comfortable."

"You haven't seen my kitchen yet." Absently, he fingered her renegade cowlick. "You're in for a treat."

She *had* seen his kitchen, but decided it was best not to share that knowledge with him.

CHAPTER 10

I paint objects as I think them, not as I see them.
– Picasso

A half hour later, David, Ashley and Pickle stood in Frank's Pizza, waiting for a pepperoni pizza. From what Ashley had learned from the residents, Frank's Pizza was not just the local pizzeria, it was the *only* pizzeria in town. The restaurant was empty except for a teen boy tossing pizza dough behind the counter, and David remarked that the air-conditioning was a welcome respite from the afternoon heat.

She stepped to the vending machine near the exit. "Do you want a candy bar to tide you over until we get back to your cabin? I need a sugar fix."

"I can wait another few minutes."

"I can't." With that declaration, she plunked three quarters into the machine. She waited for her choice to drop to the shelf at the bottom, but the candy bar kept dangling from the release mechanism. Muttering, she banged on the side. Nothing.

She began shaking the machine. "David?"

"Careful. It might topple, and the glass will break." He strode over, the pizza box balanced in one hand and Pickle's leash in the other.

"My candy bar is stuck, and I lost three quarters."

He sighed, set the box on an empty table, and secured Pickle's leash to a chair leg. "This can only happen to you."

"Help."

"Wait a couple seconds. Be patient. The machine might sense your candy bar hasn't dropped."

She tapped her foot. "Nothing is happening."

"Here." He dug into his pocket and handed her more quarters. "Try again and select the same candy bar. Maybe it will jerk yours loose."

She did as he suggested. Nothing changed.

She crouched to peer up into the machine. "The flap is stuck. Now you've lost your quarters too."

He cocked his head, considering the machine, then reached in his pocket. "This is the last of my quarters. Choose another candy bar from the row above."

"Grand idea." She inserted the quarters, made her selection, then exhaled. "Sadly, it isn't working."

"Right. Okay. Let's shake the machine. You take one side; I'll take the other."

No amount of jostling dislodged the candy bar.

"I wish I had those frozen chocolate cookies from the other day," he said, once they were back in his truck and following the road to his cabin. "They might alleviate your chocolate craving."

"Where are the cookies?"

He grinned. "I ate most of them. You're right, they're much better frozen. I refroze the rest."

"Frozen, thawed, and refrozen? David!" She sputtered in righteous exasperation.

After they parked in his driveway, he pressed a kiss on her forehead. "There are cookies left."

"You're trying to placate me."

"Maybe."

Before he opened her door, she jumped from his truck, the dog at her heels, and grabbed a Frisbee off the ground.

"Fetch, Pickle!" She threw the Frisbee across the lawn, and Pickle gleefully dashed after it. The sky was a dazzling blue, the sun blinding overhead. She enjoyed the radiant heat and had grown accustomed to it, though she would've welcomed a breeze. The air was motionless.

"Let's feast on pizza, then plan a walk after dinner," David said.

"Do you know what I have to say about that?" Amidst a cluster of buttery-yellow dandelions, she plucked a fluffy sphere and poised it before her lips.

"What?" He stepped closer and squinted at her, shading his eyes from the sun's glare.

She took a hearty lungful of air and puffed, sending delicate cottony seeds through the air.

He laughed and ducked. "What's that for?"

She blew again.

Another shout of his laughter almost drowned out her reply. "For making fun of me in the pizza parlor when I lost my quarters."

"You nearly broke the vending machine with your muscling."

"Muscling? Muscling?" Delighted she could make him laugh, she softened her voice and cooed, "The machine eats quarters and stole our money."

"We're the ones who put the money in to begin with." He set the pizza box on the ground and regarded Pickle, who had discovered a cool spot under the massive oak tree in the side yard. The dog's newfound Frisbee lay beside him. "Blame it on a machine malfunction."

"Sure, stick up for the vending machine instead of me."

David moved so swiftly she didn't have time to react, save for a surprised screech as he plucked a handful of fluffy dandelions.

"Now David, I assume you're not childish enough to retaliate."

"Do you recognize the foolishness of needling someone who is bigger and smarter than you?" he asked.

"Hah! You wish!" She hurled her hands to her hips. "Absolutely not."

He chased her to the oak tree, and she picked dandelions while she ran and flung them at him. Her shrieks of laughter sounded across his secluded acreage.

When he caught her, his boyish smile sent her pulse reeling. A bead of sweat trickled down his forehead, and she wiped it with her forefinger.

"You're a treasure, Ashley Madden." He brought her into his arms, and their laughter faded, replaced by a deep kiss.

She gazed past him, eyeing the oak tree. Somewhere overhead, a robin chirped. "David?"

"Hmm?"

"That tree is ideal for climbing. The branches are low-hanging and sturdy."

"Don't even think about it."

ONCE INSIDE THE CABIN, Ashley yanked off her boots and set her tote bag on the redwood chair. She filled Pickle's water bowl at the sink while David grabbed cold drinks, plates, and silverware from the kitchen cabinets. He excused himself to freshen up and reappeared minutes later, wearing denim shorts and pulling on a white T-shirt. Her breathing stopped as she stared at his bare chest and broad-shouldered physique. The magazine photos of him had pictured him unfairly. In person, he displayed a reserved strength and a strong allure that film couldn't capture.

He gave her one of his devastatingly lazy smiles, and she scolded herself for allowing her mind to wander where it had no business wandering.

I'm falling in love with him.

Panic bumped. What? No. Never.

David Fodero is infinitely appealing.

Yes, but...

David Fodero basked in a wealthy Manhattan lifestyle she could hardly fathom. He was unreachable, unattainable, and altogether out of her league.

"Quite the kitchen, David," she joked, clamping down her emotions. "Vintage is a suitable adjective." She adjusted the faucet and splashed cold water on her cheeks. She dried her face with a clean towel, then spun to arrange the place settings on the wooden table. A window overlooked the unaffected rural surroundings. A grassy meadow beyond evoked a scene from a different era.

"Everything here is marvelous," she added. Beyond marvelous. His park-like location brought to mind temperate summer days spent resting in a hammock and reading the Bible.

He stepped to her, pulling her close to his chest. "I can see the stars at night."

"It must be beautiful." She smiled, trying to contain her growing tenderness for him.

"So you like the kitchen?" A faint catch in his voice disarmed her. He was always so self-assured, yet he valued her opinion.

"Stone floors and blue cabinets." She twisted and discovered he was studying her. "What's not to like?"

"Nothing." He offered a self-indulgent grin. "My kitchen has periodic appeal."

"Perhaps an acquired taste, and it may lack a little... modernization. Let's begin with the yellow stove and blue oven."

"Yellow and blue don't match?" He reached for two green speckled ceramic cups from the cabinet, then opened the refrigerator for an energy drink and a sugary soda.

"Stainless steel appliances are in style." She teasingly smacked him with the towel. Then, sobering, she focused on a paint splatter on the floor. "David, I have a confession."

His hand stilled for a split second before he closed the refrigerator door. "Go on."

She lifted her gaze to meet his. "I've already seen your kitchen."

"When?"

"The day I dropped off the peaches. I couldn't resist a peek." She folded the towel on the counter. Silence reigned for too many seconds.

"I'm sorry."

He poured their beverages into the cups. "Please explain."

"I was curious."

"No." His jaw was tight. "Explain why you didn't tell me sooner."

She dug her nails into her palms. "I should have. I let you down. I let myself down. Please accept my apology."

"I'm not quick to point a finger. We've all made mistakes and I'm grateful for your honesty. It means a great deal to me."

She drew back slightly. "All is forgiven?"

"All is forgiven."

Because of the lump in her throat, she couldn't form any

words. She picked up Pickle's water dish and stepped into the living room.

"The stove is a cast iron antique," David said from the kitchen. "I'll grant the oven might require replacing, although it heats up to temperature."

"What temperature?"

"Two hundred degrees Fahrenheit."

"That's not hot." She set Pickle's dish down. "Do you bake?"

"Never. There's a tasty bakery in town, though."

She rolled her eyes in humorous exasperation. "Spoken like a true guy."

"I'm practical," he called out. "Why replace a working appliance?"

"I see. You're aiming for retro, whether the oven heats or not."

"I heard that. Two hundred degrees—"

"Isn't hot enough to bake a cupcake," she muttered.

She paused, noting the rusted coffee can by the fireplace. She cast a quick glance toward the kitchen, then grasped the can and peeked inside. Two dollar bills lay crumpled at the bottom.

David strode into the living room, sipping from his speckled cup. "Ashley, do you prefer your soft drink in here?"

"I'm fine for now. Thanks."

He stopped. Swallowed. Propped a shoulder against the doorjamb. "What are you doing?"

She held up the coffee can, regretting the timing of his entrance. "I'm sorry. I didn't mean to snoop—"

"You did, though." His face became expressionless, his voice sharp in contrast.

She set the can back down. Tears stung her eyes. "I said I was sorry."

"C'mere." He set his cup on the table and beckoned her to sit on the sofa.

"What about the pizza?"

"I prefer cold pizza. I hope you do too." He raked a hand through his hair. "I didn't intend to charge you with a crime for picking up a rusty old can."

She planned to answer when she was good and ready. She planned to sit when she was good and ready. But there was no contest when it came to David's quiet apology.

She perched on the edge of the sofa. "Sometimes, you are thoroughly impossible."

"Others have said the same. I'm working on becoming a better person. I make excuses, though I try to take full responsibility for my words and actions."

She had leftover anger to challenge him. Nevertheless, she wasn't *that* upset. Besides, she was a Christian and granted forgiveness graciously. Nor could she ignore the mindlessness of upsetting their precious minutes with a needless misunderstanding.

He settled on the sofa and requested she sit closer. Once she scooted near, he slung an arm around her shoulders. "We've spent hours together, yet we're virtual strangers in many respects."

After all their banter, an upscale dinner, and endless delightful kisses, they were still strangers?

Still, she bestowed her best smile. "More sharing? You go first."

"Why am I always first?"

"Because you owe me a candy bar, and the suggestion is yours."

He kept his gaze on the fireplace. "Are you ready for more accounts of my artistic struggle?"

Stunned and flattered because he'd relented so quickly, she nodded. He was a private man, yet he chose to share his personal stories with her. And she sensed that this story held special significance for him.

"Did you ever hold on to something that meant the world to you, even though it carried little monetary value?" He smiled, and the curious tug on her heart occurred again, that tender odd ache.

"A rusty coffee can?" she teased.

"The can is a symbol."

"For what?"

"Do you recall when I told you the road to success is built on hard work?" His tone was strangely hoarse.

"And you mentioned it takes years and years."

He stared at the can. Abundant silence. With David, she was learning patience.

"When I attended NYU…"

"You were awarded a full scholarship." She patted his forearm, a congratulatory pat he probably considered sophomoric. Still, their relationship was tentative, though for her, it was on the verge of becoming more serious with each of his tales. "Your family must've been proud and thrilled." She switched to an encouraging note.

His features remained somber, and she doubted his father had sent any gratifying *"Atta boys"* his way.

Every minute she spent with David, she understood him more. He was complex. He was smart and talented. And he'd been hurt. His recollections brought a broader comprehension of his nature. He was kind, yet vulnerable.

"A scholarship doesn't compensate for everything." His voice deepened. "Tuition and books, sure, though not the infinite art supplies."

She nodded in commiseration. "I can't operate without the countless paintbrushes and watercolors I resupply for my studio each month."

"Nor did my scholarship pay for meals and living costs."

She looked up at him. "Your parents didn't help you financially?"

"My father didn't want his son to become an artist, remember?" David reached for his cup and sipped. "He was pleased about the scholarship. Nonetheless, I was on my own."

She sat engrossed, listening to every sentence, every tenuous shade of David's voice. She had learned already that whenever he mentioned his father, aloofness laced his expression. In this case, she suspected his father's reaction had hurt David the most. She considered remarking that his father's disinterest was cruel, for it had deeply wounded his talented, impressionable son. However, she reserved judgment. "How did you earn money in college?"

"I staked out busy street corners and sketched people. I carried a stool, drawing paper, charcoal pencils, and a kneaded eraser."

"An artist's favorite friend," she agreed. "The eraser doesn't leave any heavy marks behind."

"Hurray. A woman who knows art." He kissed the top of her forehead. "I charged five dollars for each portrait."

A portrait that now commanded over a thousand dollars.

"The key to drawing a good portrait is shading and proper proportions." His smile quickened her heart. Art was, first and foremost, a passion for him. "The distance between the nose and mouth is important."

"You sketched in the middle of busy New York?" She visualized him as a young man, alone in a city of eight million people.

"At the intersection of Broadway and West Forty-First Street, just south of Times Square." His answer was matter of fact, though his arm tightened around her. "I displayed the coffee can in a conspicuous spot for tips. I was an emerging artist developing my craft while earning money at the same time."

"Very enterprising."

"The first two dollars I ever earned are in that coffee can." He ran his thumb around the rim of his cup. "A gray-haired grandmother came by on my first day and requested I sketch her granddaughter. When I finished, I thought the granddaughter's teeth were too white of a contrast, though they seemed pleased. The can is a reminder to celebrate the triumphs, no matter how small."

He'd saved his first tip and carried the money with him all these years. Ashley wrestled with the explosive emotions welling in her chest.

She blinked back tears and searched his face. His expression was carefully aloof.

Be proud, she thought. *Embrace your God-given talent. Never second-guess yourself.*

Lightly, she touched his hand. "That grandmother must've recognized your tremendous ability."

"I doubt it, though I value your compliment." He set down his cup, lifted her hair and nuzzled her nape.

Ashley rested her head on his shoulder and propped her feet on the coffee table. He held her close.

She drew a fortifying breath, reluctant to shatter the intimate mood. Nevertheless, she plunged ahead. "I noticed your vision loss."

He shifted positions. "How can you tell?"

"When you look at me, you favor a certain side. Plus, your reference to a deaf Beethoven the first day we met, coupled with Cherish's rumor mill."

"Am I completely transparent?"

"In times of trouble, we all reach out, whether we realize it or not. You did when you alluded to Beethoven. What happened to you?"

He sighed. "More than enough questions about me."

She almost flinched at the brusqueness in his tone.

His unwarranted flippancy grated on her. How could they not discuss what was so significant to him? Wasn't he the person who had declared not ten minutes earlier that they were virtual strangers?

"Please don't brush off the topic," she replied. "I want to identify with what's important to you. Don't stop painting. You're too talented."

"Thanks for the encouragement." He shoved a throw pillow aside, stood, and reached for her hand. "Let's eat the pizza before it gets cold."

"I thought you preferred cold pizza."

"I changed my mind."

"You're dismissing me."

"I'm dismissing the subject because I refuse to allow an in-depth analysis of my vision loss. Not to anyone except my physician. Not even you." He succeeded in displaying a semblance of a smile. "Come into the kitchen. I prefer to dine with a lovely companion rather than eating alone."

CHAPTER 11

Youth has no age.
– Picasso

*A*s they ate their pizza, sitting across from each other at the kitchen table after she'd whispered a prayer of grace, David was courteous, yet pensive. When they finished, she cleared their dishes, stacked them in the sink, and discarded the paper napkins in the trash.

"No dishwasher?" She tried for an easy-going conversation, hoping he'd bounce back from his contemplative mood.

"I prefer to wash dishes by hand," he replied.

His profile was silhouetted in the glow of the afternoon sun gleaming through the window. His hands were jammed in his pockets, and Pickle relaxed by his feet. A jug of water still sat on the table. She'd sliced lime and lemon into the water for flavor, and two half-filled glasses of water remained.

She started for the living room, intending to pull on her

hiking boots, then ask him to drive her back to the inn. The walk he'd mentioned? Well, they wouldn't be taking a walk anytime soon.

He balled up a napkin she'd missed collecting. "A few months ago," he said softly, "I woke up and discovered I'd lost vision in one eye."

She stopped.

Ignoring the solid beating of her heart, she padded into the kitchen and seated herself at the table again. He sat across from her.

"This subject is difficult for me." He held out his hand. She grasped it and gave a supportive squeeze.

More than a little unnerved, her thoughts spun, one in particular. When she'd studied for her art degree, she happened upon a quote by Pablo Picasso, the renowned Spanish painter and sculptor.

"'Others have seen what is and asked why,'" she quoted. "'I have seen what could be and asked why not.'"

"Picasso," David replied.

With a vague sense of foreboding, she refilled their water glasses. "Maybe I can help you."

"I don't need anyone's help." His dark eyebrows snapped together. "I'm explaining because you pressed me for details."

She hadn't but didn't argue. Stiffening, she shoved her chair back.

Pickle came to his feet and stared up at her.

"Point taken, David," she said. "Loud and clear. I'm leaving and phoning an Uber."

Because the point *was* taken. Now she finally understood.

David enjoyed spending time with her, but she wasn't allowed any closer than a shared pizza. *Virtual strangers.* She'd been an amusing diversion when he was wearied, an excuse for procrastination when he was supposed to be working on a commissioned painting.

137

He stood, shadowing her. He placed his hands on her shoulders. "Please stay."

Her heartbeat doubled at the despair in his voice, though her tolerance and patience had worn thin. Only a fool would keep listening, conscious of being used as a sounding board because there was no one else.

She swiveled toward the living room.

"Ashley." His voice came from behind her. "Forgive my abruptness."

She whirled. "You drive me away when I want to support you." She seized her tote bag and fished for her cellphone. "I'm a silly art teacher and will never meet your lofty standards to—"

He reached her in two steps and gently caught her wrist. "Don't go."

She jerked from his grip.

"I've got cookies in the freezer." His pleading tone, his grasping for something to keep her near—cookies, of all things—demolished her anger. Undecided whether to laugh or cry, she did both.

He cradled her, kissed her neck, her lips, and wiped the tears from her cheeks. She didn't resist. She couldn't resist. She was falling in love with a man who was creative, enterprising, skeptical, and in many ways reminded her of the enchanting, vulnerable students she taught—all seeking support.

He rested his chin on the top of her head. "I don't deserve someone as sweet and caring as you in my life."

"I'm here," she whispered, and buried her face in his chest. His heart beat fast and solid against her cheek.

He led her into the living room, to the sofa, and circled his arm around her. She sank down beside him, picking up a throw pillow that had fallen to the floor. Pickle took up his usual spot by the fireplace.

"My condition is called NAION, an abbreviation for a lengthy description," David began. "Non-arteritic anterior ischemic optic neuropathy."

"You expect me to remember that?" She smiled, eager to ease a challenging conversation.

Her teasing did the trick, because he chuckled. "In summary, there's a loss of blood flow from my optic nerve leading to the brain."

"Were you in pain when it happened?"

"No. I'm not in pain now, either."

Her smile wavered. "What causes the condition?"

"My doctor in New York referred me to numerous studies citing high blood pressure and/or smoking. Neither applies to me."

"What is your doctor's treatment recommendation?"

"Nothing, except for daily aspirin and a healthy lifestyle. Usually, the condition doesn't get any worse."

She placed a hand on his forearm. "This is encouraging news."

"Nor does it get any better."

She winced. "Will wearing eyeglasses help?"

"No. Eyeglasses aid nearsightedness or farsightedness but won't restore a damaged optic nerve. The doctor assured me that my brain will adjust, and it has."

"Oh, David, I'm sincerely sorry." A thought arose, one she blurted before fully considering. "Is your other eye affected?"

"There's a 30 percent chance. Luckily, my vision is twenty-twenty in that eye."

Thrown off balance, she echoed half to herself, "A 30 percent chance."

"I'm absolutely fine." He gave her a cheerful smile she didn't believe for a minute.

"Really?"

"Really."

"Is your vision loss the reason you aren't painting?" She wavered to steady herself and pace her questions. "You're known for being prolific."

"I can still paint."

"But you're not."

He shrugged. "I'm a realist, and not a very productive one."

"Perhaps you've set impossibly high standards for yourself." *Much like what she'd been accused of doing with her ex-boyfriend.*

"Perhaps." David released a heavy sigh. "Time will tell, though I imagine my painting has changed."

"Change is good."

He rubbed a fist over his jaw. "Sometimes."

"Prayer is better." She kept her hand on his forearm. "Will you pray with me?"

"You pray. I'll listen."

She bowed her head, and David did the same.

"Dear Lord, David is becoming a new creation," she whispered. "Please make way in his mind for fresh prospects and habits. Some of your greatest miracles are created when people are in transition. Encourage David through this difficult period and grant him wisdom and peace. Give him faith to comprehend. Amen."

David lifted his head. "I admit I feel better."

"It's not me. It's God." She raised her palms to heaven. "He promised He will never leave us or forsake us. Take heart in His assurances."

"I'll try."

Unlike the past hour's ups and downs, the next few minutes passed serenely. She relaxed in the comfortable surroundings, a dog by the fireplace, the special man she'd fallen for holding her as if he'd never let go.

A sharp pang of longing went through her. This restful,

contented life was a life she'd never live. She wanted children someday. However, children necessitated marriage and a husband, and neither was part of her future.

David pressed a kiss to her temple. "Now I want to hear more about you."

"Me?" She leaned back.

"Why did Sarah call you Twinkle?"

Something about his engaging smile prodded her to answer. After all, he'd spoken with honesty and openness.

"I've always gotten excited about my students' drawings," she said.

He threw her a speculative grin. "Please continue."

"A few years ago, an adorable autistic boy remarked that my eyes twinkled like sparkly green stars after I'd praised him. He is wonderfully artistic."

"How old is he?"

"Ten." She crossed her feet. "These kids appreciate art. They're my type of people."

"I appreciate art."

She nudged his rib with her elbow. "Therefore, it goes without saying…"

"I'm your type of person. I'm flattered, Twinkle."

She grinned. "Are you making fun of me?"

"Never."

"In summary, the name stuck. My close friends use my nickname often."

"Twinkle, twinkle, you are my shining star."

Heat hastened her pulse at his tender words and heavy-lidded gaze. Surely a man capable of evoking such profound emotions through his paintings wasn't teasing any longer.

Regardless, she wouldn't be drawn in by an artist who was brilliant, funny, and so attractive that her temperature rose ten degrees the moment she set eyes on him.

No, no. Surely, she wouldn't be a pathetic fool a second

time—charmed by a man feigning interest, then dropping her when he found a more appealing woman.

That is, unless that particular man began kissing her with such abandon, cuddling her, his lips caressing hers so urgently her heart responded with intense longing.

Minutes after their kisses ended, he didn't take his gaze from her face as he invited her back into the kitchen.

She lifted a teasing eyebrow. "For cookies?"

"We could eat a box, although I want to paint you first."

"I thought you were using the photograph by the river to paint me."

"You're here in person. What could be better?"

They exchanged smiles.

"I'll take the dog out and grab some special paints I store in my truck," he said.

She perched on the edge of a kitchen chair and waited. He returned carrying an assortment of flamboyant shades of blue and red paint, gold glitter, a brush, and a sea sponge. An old T-shirt cut up as a rag was tucked into the waistband of his shorts.

Her gaze narrowed. "Where's your canvas?"

"Don't need one."

"Aren't you going to paint me?"

And then she realized it. He intended to literally paint *her*.

"Um, nope." She jumped up and backed away. "No dice." It hadn't occurred to her beforehand because the idea was absolutely, utterly insane. "Find someone else to paint."

He looked around. "Who?"

"Call one of your Hollywood models."

"None hold a candle to you." He approached her with the sponge and a pot of cobalt-blue paint. "This is water soluble and will wash off."

"Your assurances are supposed to appease me?" She gazed at the ceiling, searching for a guarantee somewhere, anywhere. "You lured me into the kitchen because I assumed we were eating cookies."

"We can. I have a half box left."

"That's all?"

"I'll spare you a couple."

She lunged for the freezer, pulling open the door, but he was faster. He set down the sponge and paint and snagged the box.

She peered into the freezer. "Where's your frozen pizzas and peanut butter ice cream?"

"I don't eat junk food."

"Yeah, right. What kind of guy doesn't eat Hungry-Man dinners?"

"Me." He held the cookie box over her head. "Shall we eat these now or later?"

She blew out the air stuck in her throat. "Let's wait."

"Wise choice. Body art is fascinating, and you're an inspiration, Ashley."

She cast a sideways glance toward the doorway. "I'll agree under one condition."

"Conditions, now?"

"Absolutely. You paint my face, and I'll paint yours."

"Agreed. Stand still." He tapped the sponge into the paint, then dabbed numerous drops on her cheeks. "Remember, don't sweat."

"On the hottest day of the year?"

"The air-conditioning is on."

"Great. Until I step outside into the eighty-degree heat and humidity."

She curved toward the window, eager to view her reflection in the glass. Her blue cheeks were muted, giving her the appearance of a lopsided clown.

"Ninety-nine percent of people who are body painted say they would do it again." David spoke calmly, his actions

143

focused, as he guided her around to face him. He stood back, then applied a dab of gold glitter on her nose. "Excellent!"

"This calls for retaliation." She flipped him a smile, snatched the sponge, and aimed for his forehead. A blob of gold glitter dripped from his chin when she missed. "Sorry." She reached for the blue paint and knocked over the pot, splattering paint across the stone floor.

"I might need to renovate the kitchen after all." He drew her to him and kissed her. "It's also been noted that face painting unites people."

"Where did you read that?"

"Somewhere."

Yes, he was impossible.

In a lushly renovated cabin in the woods, their laughter rang out.

Pickle barked and raced around them. Frozen cookies were left to thaw.

And all was perfect in Ashley's world.

CHAPTER 12

The chief enemy of creativity is good sense.
- Picasso

The following two days passed in a blur. Ashley notified Nancy at the art gallery, reporting that she'd found David and he was all right. She didn't reveal his eyesight loss. The subject was personal and up to him to explain.

Ashley phoned the leader of the fellowship group at her church that evening. "I'll drive back to my apartment on Saturday, so I'm prepared to teach Sunday School," she told her.

Then she texted her substitute teachers and was assured her students were doing splendidly.

Taking maximum advantage of their days together, David invited her to peruse the boutiques in town, and dine with him at respective restaurants including The Garden Terrace, recognized for their mesquite barbecued ribs and sugar-free lemon cake, both of which delighted Ashley.

She wore light summer dresses, thankfully she'd packed several, as she had the tendency to over-pack. From Sarah, she borrowed flirty straw hats and applied black mascara to bring out her large hazel eyes. Friends had remarked that her eyes were her best feature, so why not accentuate them?

During a shopping trip to Aaron's Art Shop, David insisted on purchasing hundreds of dollars' worth of supplies for her studio. They left the shop with their arms laden with bags, and Pickle walked with them on a secure leash as they crossed the street to David's truck.

Ashley sighed. "I wanted to reach my exercise quota by working out at the inn's gym. Julian told me he recently updated with state-of-the-art equipment."

David deposited their bags into his trunk. "*Wanted* to reach your goals?"

"Yes, that's the key word. I haven't visited the gym once."

"At least your intentions are good." His eyes crinkled at the corners. "I owe you an excursion to Juniper Mountain and the hiking trip I promised the other day."

"You're referring to the day we ate pizza in your cabin?"

He shut the trunk and took hold of Pickle's leash. "The very same."

"And the day you painted me."

"Yup."

She accepted his outstretched hand. "Despite your assurances concerning water-soluble paint, Julian definitely gave me an odd look when I arrived back at the inn."

"You washed the paint off in my bathroom before I drove you to the inn."

She tilted her head. "Yes, I did. Lots of scrubbing and rubbing alcohol helped remove the paint, but the gold glitter insisted on sticking to my nose."

He kissed the tip of her nose. "Lucky for you, all the paint has worn off now."

"Lucky for *you,* or I would've cheerfully thrown you out of a tree."

"If you recall, I don't climb trees anymore."

"There's always a second time."

He chuckled and stopped in midstep. "That's something else I love about you. You always express exactly what's on your mind."

Something else he loved.

Her heart cartwheeled in her chest. David spoke about love.

She stared into his arresting gaze. For a number of seconds, she permitted herself to wonder what it would be like to be loved by this artistic, enigmatic man? They'd spend hours together, conversing about art, wisecracking, and relishing each other's company.

I'll help you confront your vision problem, she thought. *I'll lend support at every crossroad, and you can show my precious students your exquisite canvases and provide expert tips. We'll attend concerts—maybe the music of Percy Grainger. We'll serve in church. We'll pray.*

Where, exactly? In Cherish? In New York City? In Greenwood?

He cupped her chin, smoothing his thumb along her jawline. His woodsy, male scent floated to her nostrils, prompting an intense awareness of the vital man bending his head to kiss her.

Right there. In the middle of the main street.

From the first second she'd met him, her feelings had been overwhelming. No matter how light-hearted their conversations, a kiss invariably followed. Around David, she was comfortable, and everything seemed familiar. With him she felt cared for and safe.

"You're very special, Ashley." His voice lowered to a murmur. "Never forget that."

His deep tone blended with the hum of residents chatting among themselves. A mother chased after a toddler who lifted his shirt over his head as he ran across the sidewalk. On the grassy lawn of the park, children invented a game, legs churning as they ran in circles.

A life worth living. A life with David. A wonderful, fanciful dream.

She recalled the sting of heartbreak, the crushing, biting wound, and she determinedly shoved her dreams aside. She'd been hurt by a man once, her fantasies shattered, and she wouldn't risk it again. Besides, no one fell in love in mere days.

Did they?

They continued their wanderings to Whitney's, the local ice cream parlor. She ordered a chocolate sundae topped with hot fudge and a cherry, and David selected a triple decker coffee cone. Pet-friendly, the owners produced a natural frozen yogurt for dogs served in a bowl. Pickle's eyes grew round, and he lapped up the yogurt.

"We've gone to the dogs," the owner joked, which earned a burst of laughter.

Ashley and David assembled outside on sunny-yellow chairs, leaning their elbows on the wrought-iron table. When they couldn't eat another bite, David offered to walk her to the inn, assuring he'd double back to his truck and deliver her art supplies in the morning.

They resumed their pace, strolling hand in hand. The afternoon sun beat down on them, though a faint breeze stirred and ruffled her hair. Nevertheless, the minutes were sleepy and motionless, the air hot and aromatic. Songbirds chirped from the trees, and joggers passed them at a slow clip.

"About that invite…" David began.

"To Walnut Forest and Juniper Mountain?"

"You're a hiker. Here's your opportunity to show off your expertise." The sparkle in his gaze underscored his sheer enjoyment of joking with her.

"I hike a couple blocks around my apartment, which is on a flat sidewalk." She chuckled. "Primarily, I walk on a treadmill in my living room while I listen to audiobooks."

"What type of books?"

"I gravitate toward adventure thrillers."

They curved onto a quiet, residential lane. "We share many interests, Ashley, beginning with art and audiobooks."

She studied his face, his expressions of tenderness.

By silent agreement, they zeroed in on a park bench. "You're on a roll, David. Please continue."

"Continue what?"

"Listing our interests."

He pressed a kiss on her cheek. "Exercise is another."

She jabbed him with her elbow. "I haven't found the time because I'm spending every waking minute with you. Therefore, it's all your fault I've gained weight this week."

"My fault?" He held a hand over his heart. "I'll willingly accept the blame, honored you'd use me as an excuse."

His good humor erased any reservations for missing her workouts, and she couldn't contain her joking. "As well you should."

"Set aside an hour each day," he said. "Mornings work best for me."

"Your suggestion takes discipline, which I evidently lack."

"You're the most disciplined woman I've ever met. You operate your own studio, you're clearly excellent with children, and your inspirational words shine with conviction."

His observations floored her. She flipped back her thick hair that kept falling over her eyes and studied him. God's purpose was to redeem and rebuild. It wasn't too late for David's faith to be restored.

"The old has gone, the new is here." She referenced a passage from Corinthians.

David grinned. "Make way for the new." His grin widened, his eyes an electric, luminous blue. In its depths, she lost herself in her expectations, her imaginings, her emotions.

She recalled the first day they met at his cabin and formally shook hands. Every part of her senses had fixated on the touch of his calloused fingers linked with hers. He reminded her of the fictional heroes she adored, a resilient, charismatic male. A protagonist straight from a storybook, complete with a happily ever after. The more hours he occupied, the more her initial observations had proved correct. David Fodero could overcome any obstacle, if only his faith and optimism were reinforced.

She pondered a second possibility. Should anything happen and he lost eyesight in his good eye—Well, she couldn't permit her thoughts to go there.

An artist who couldn't see. An artist who couldn't paint.

No.

Nevertheless, uncertainties persisted.

What if?

Her internal response was immediate. *Trust God.*

David shouldn't allow his hardships to prevent him from appreciating what God had planted inside him. Every person was unique and special. Every person had something in them to help press through their adversities and reach the other side.

So deep in thought, she didn't hear David's question at first. "Have you ever gone camping?" he asked again.

She viewed the inn, visible up ahead. "When I was eight years old, I camped overnight with my father and an elderly couple from our church. They'd been married for decades and were schoolteachers. They were reaching retirement age and wanted to serve the Lord by volunteering."

"Did they retire?"

"Yes, and they were excited to offer their unique gifts of support and mentoring children in a remote country. They were Christians and believed giving their lives to God helped to change people."

David picked up his steps and steered her toward a park bench beneath a large magnolia tree. The shade from the fragrant pink blossoms offered a welcome respite from the heat, and Pickle chose a place in the cool grass.

"How did your camping expedition go?" David secured the dog's leash to a tree and grabbed Pickle's striped elephant from his pocket, tossing it to him.

"Camping was an adventure." Ashley settled on the bench, the cool iron pressing against her bare legs. She was grateful she'd worn a casual outfit—cotton shorts, a white eyelet blouse, and sandals. "My father and I prayed with our friends and asked God to mark their journey with safety."

"Sometimes, I miss church."

She touched his wrist, hearing the desire in his deep voice. "Church misses you."

"I'm struggling. You rely on God and never lose faith."

"I've lost faith more often than I can count, beginning with the camping trip."

"Hard to believe."

Seconds ticked.

She expelled a breath, knowing he waited for a reply.

"The married couple was scheduled to devote the upcoming six months to a mountain village overseas, though the wife expressed reservations. There had been recent news reports that the impoverished country was suffering an unanticipated upheaval. I talked them into traveling."

"You?"

"They planned to do so much good and spread the word of the Lord."

Happy remembrances of the tan canvas tents erected side by side, sitting around the campfire toasting marshmallows over a sizzling fire, brought fond memories.

At least initially.

"When did they return from their missionary trip?" David's question pulled her out of her musings and yanked her back to reality. "Are you still in touch with them?"

"No." She choked on the single word.

"Why? What happened?"

"They were killed. Guerillas attacked their village late at night and none of the townspeople and missionaries survived." She swiped at the tears forming at the corner of her eyes. "For months afterwards, I blamed myself."

The warmth of David's reassuring fingers lifted the weight off her chest. "An attack in a foreign country is hardly your fault."

Pickle inched toward them, and she picked him up, allowing him to lick her arms. "I was the person who encouraged them to go on the trip."

"You were eight years old. It's unlikely you influenced their decision."

"I still believed it was all my fault, and my convictions faltered. My father uplifted me, brought me to church, prayed with me at night." She sucked in a lungful of oxygen. "I remember the wife read stories from the Bible that night we were camping. They were righteous, kind Christians."

David leaned closer. "What kind of stories?"

"She spoke about Paul's thorn in the flesh from 2 Corinthians 12:7." While Ashley recited the verse, David trained his gaze on Pickle.

"When I was young, I studied the New Testament and memorized favorite passages," he replied.

"Do you remember the significance of Paul's story?"

"There are many theories." David repositioned himself and faced her. He was so close his legs brushed against hers. "Recollections of Paul's past, former temptations, or perhaps a physical ailment."

"Paul's eyesight, his difficulty seeing, is a possibility often examined." She adjusted Pickle so he wouldn't slide off her lap. "Sometimes God uses our physical weaknesses to humble us."

"I'm hardly a saint, Ashley. You're comparing my eyesight loss to Paul's thorn?"

His question hung in the silence between them. In his tone, she heard defensiveness and despair.

She instructed herself to breathe, and slanted a glance toward him. He didn't meet her gaze.

Who was she to judge him if he was bitter at God? Was she a better Christian?

The sun lowered behind a cloud and softened David's rigid features. She breathed in a bottomless breath, saturated with the scent of fragrant magnolias.

She took his hand. "I'm truly sorry about your vision loss, David."

Absently, he scratched Pickle's head and stared at the empty lot across the road. "I appreciate your concern."

"Remember God's grace and know it is enough. Walk through your season of uncertainty and praise Him. His power is made perfect through our weaknesses."

"Once, I believed. When adolescence kicked in, I questioned everything." He met her gaze for a split-second before refocusing on the lot. "Despite my mother's prodding, I never returned to church."

"How many years has it been?"

"Two decades."

Her lips parted in astonishment. "Yet you're commissioned to paint a church."

"The exterior." He shifted. "Not the interior."

She envisioned him as a young boy, as an adolescent, and her heart fluttered at the image. Fresh-faced, probably skinny with long arms and legs. He craved love and protection and assurance. Quiet and reserved, with a spark of creative mischief. Even when attending elementary school, his artistic ability must have spilled from every pore, although he had recognized his father's displeasure.

She formed her lips into a smile. "Are you sorry you accepted the commission?"

"It brought me to Cherish. It brought me to you."

Her movements never faltered as she placed the dog on the ground, though her emotions spun in a thousand directions. She stared up at David's face, felt the familiar strength of his strong arms as he cuddled her.

Her heart burst with something she could only identify as love.

She longed to vocalize her feelings because she agreed with him. Come what may, their meeting each other had been predestined.

Although no. It had been calculated. By her.

Her throat tightened, and her voice was snatched away.

"Your emotions are written all over your face, Ashley." David seemed unaware of the tears threatening to blur her own vision. "You're an open book."

"Am I?" She drove a hand through her hair, tempted to pat down her rambunctious cowlick, which surely must be sticking straight up in this humidity. She didn't, because David patted it down for her.

"I knew it the moment you showed up at my cabin wearing sandals, searching for a mountain located in another state." A grin tugged at his full mouth. "The expression on your face was a definite giveaway."

A giveaway for her stupidity, she chastised herself. Again, she sent a prayer to God to forgive her for deceiving David.

She shoved to her feet. "I should tell you something."

"No climbing trees, I hope." He stood and unleashed Pickle. "Although I'm accepting options for tomorrow's plans."

"It's not about tomorrow."

And just like that, she lost her nerve, refusing to deflate the shining admiration for her in his gaze.

"What is it?" he asked.

"I can't. I should spend the day packing since I'm planning to leave on Saturday."

His gaze narrowed. He grabbed her hand. "You're leaving so soon?"

"David, I've been in Cherish almost a week."

He stared down at their fingers, firmly entwined. "You can't stay any longer?"

"My students miss me, and I miss them. In addition, I'm in charge of a Sunday school class at my church. I love teaching five-year-old's about God. Besides, I imagine you've neglected your commission because you've invested all your hours with me."

"I've been painting."

"Great! The centennial portrait?"

He paused, forcing her to pause, too. "A subject far more important to me."

His heated gaze robbed her of any ability to form a coherent sentence. She yearned for more, a pledge that he'd phone, a promise to see her, although he hadn't offered any commitment. None at all. Nothing.

Did he even know where she lived? She riffled through their conversations. He'd never asked. She'd never told him.

She didn't press. She didn't wish to become another conquest. Yet the intensity of how much she cared for him already scared her.

She focused on the scattered sunlight dappling through the tree leaves. An artist's eye would be scrutinizing the sun's position, the contour of the spaces where the light shone through, the elevation of the tree canopy.

David looped an arm around her shoulders. "Instead of packing, will you go to the Renaissance Faire with me?"

Taken aback, she gaped. Had she imagined his invitation?

"I have it on excellent authority, specifically yours, that you're not a fan of Renaissance Faires," she said.

"You're a fan, which is all that matters."

"You're not exactly the most sociable guy on the planet."

"I like people."

"Who?"

"You. Very much. It's the silliness involved in dressing up as a character from the fourteenth century that I object to." He held up a hand. "Don't ask, because I won't be wearing any costume."

She eyed him from head to toe. "I envision you as a knight."

He gave a gallant bow. "And you're my lady. We'll eat, drink, and watch a jousting match."

A Renaissance Faire. At last. Her veins hummed with excitement. She steeled herself not to react, but wrapped her hands around his nape, anyway. "I'm so excited, David."

"My pleasure. Let's seal our date."

Happily, she obliged, a treasured kiss beneath a Carolina-blue sky.

Savor every minute, she told herself. Someday, she'd look back upon this wondrous week with joy. A summer to remember. A summer to cherish. Days filled with brilliance and wonder and David. This cynical, witty, artistic, generous man.

She'd miss him terribly after they parted. Nonetheless, she'd provide a clear and simple explanation for why she'd initially come to Cherish. Sure, it was easier to flee than cope with her wrongdoing, but their relationship insisted she push past her fear and risk seeing the disappointment on his face.

Her jaw set, her mind made up. Though her stomach pitched at the thought, she'd tell him the truth tomorrow, at day's end.

And then she would pray, intending to make peace with her failings.

CHAPTER 13

Colors, like features, follow the changes in emotions.
- Picasso

"I refuse to wear a metal helmet." David frowned at himself in the full-length mirror of the Renaissance Faire's costume shop. "What will people think?"

Ashley gazed at him with giggling delight. "They'll think you're ingenious and original."

Considering half the men at the Faire were also dressed as knights, David highly doubted it.

Ashley had dragged him into the first shop she'd spotted and talked him into renting a knight's costume. Of course, she hadn't literally talked him into it. The joy lighting her face was all the convincing he needed. Besides, the Faire was held in a neighboring town. They wouldn't bump into anyone they knew.

As soon as he and Ashley had stepped through the gateopening, they were hailed by a court jester sporting a three-pointed hat and ringing a tiny bell while being serenaded by an animated group of musicians playing wooden flutes and tambourines.

She brushed a piece of lint off his polo shirt collar, which peeked through the cape. "What's the definition of a brave knight without armor protection?"

"A wise, practical man who can breathe."

There was something about a guy dressed in shorts—David had refused the woolen stockings and metal chest plate—and wearing a red cape that didn't quite match.

Ashley tightened the ties around his neck. "Despite you wearing sneakers instead of pointed boots, you're still the pluckiest, most dashing knight I've ever met."

He peered down at his shoes. "How many knights are plucky?"

"None until now."

She looked adorable, standing in front of him in an emerald-green velveteen gown that brought out the green hues in her hazel eyes. His gaze glided over her figure, lingering on her slim hips.

He placed a roundelet, a headpiece of padded round rings and braided trim, atop her glossy hair. The fake jewels, satin, and gold ribbons flowing from the raised bow enhanced her understated elegance. "You are a classic beauty, Lady Jane."

She grinned at the reference to her costume, fidgeted with the pearl beading along the gown's bodice, then twirled. "You're handsome indeed, Sir Galahad, especially wearing a surcoat."

He fingered the thin cotton fabric. "Surcoat? I thought it was a cape."

"You're confusing the Renaissance era with Batman."

He burst out laughing. "You expect me to walk in this

getup? Or take in any air? I'll smother in this mesh metallic hood." He tapped on the hood to emphasize his point.

"Consider yourself lucky. At least the hem of your gown won't drag in the dirt."

He fanned himself before tugging the hood over his head. "I may sweat to death."

"You're wearing shorts. Be brave, Sir Tristan."

"I thought I was Sir Galahad."

"I'm naming all the knights at King Arthur's Round Table."

"There were hundreds of knights."

"I'll list the most memorable, Sir Lancelot."

He produced a gallant bow, then guided her out of the air-conditioned shop. Appetizing aromas of steak and mushroom pies, caramel apples, and roasted turkey legs made his mouth water. "I'm beginning to understand the attraction to these silly Faires."

"Silly?"

"Entertaining," he amended.

She grinned up at him. "Because of the noble knights and elegant ladies parading around?"

"No. Because of the delicious food."

A Renaissance Faire was an elaborate week-long affair, affording a schedule of daily events including royal jousting, comedy improvisation by a swashbuckling trio, and themed weekends such as a pirate invasion.

She tugged at his hand as they walked. "Let's order two glasses of orange soda."

"Does your sweet tooth have no bounds?"

"None at all."

"They didn't serve orange soda in the fourteen hundreds."

"Now you're a purist?" She drew herself up to her full height.

He purchased soda for her, and an iced coffee for himself.

While she perused the handmade beeswax candles at an adjoining shop, he debated whether to order roasted almonds sprinkled with cinnamon, or jalapeno.

She skipped back to him. "I'd prefer chocolate-coated."

He ordered the almonds in a cone for each of them—chocolate-coated and cinnamon, respectively. As was her custom, she thanked him, bowed her head, and whispered a prayer of grace. Even here, in the middle of a noisy, bustling crowd, she openly expressed her faith because, as she informed him, "All the food we eat is a result of God's bounty."

He nodded. Her sincere conviction was beginning to rub off on him.

She fished for a handful of chocolate nuts and fed him a couple.

"These nuts are too sweet." He groaned in feigned dismay, smirked impenitently, and snatched another handful. "If I eat any more, I might be sick."

She pushed his hand safely away from her cone. "Uh, huh."

As the afternoon passed, they meandered around the open-air booths hawking items from cloth doll patterns to plush blue dragons, inhaled cheesy French fries and sausage on a stick, and joked about who was brave enough to ride the Whirl and Hurl.

He laughed more than he'd ever laughed in his lifetime.

The reason? He was with Ashley, and she had the ability to bring joy to everyday events.

Children gravitated to her. She applauded enthusiastically while little girls, muffling giggles during a ceremony, extended deep throne curtsies, then were elevated to become ladies of the realm. "By the queen herself," Ashley congratulated the girls, which earned her unreserved smiles. Their smiles included David, which brought an endearing clutch to his heart.

Ashley picked up a pamphlet and noted that the jousting match began at three o'clock. "Let's get there early so we can snag a good seat."

"Is the jousting held outside under the blazing hot sun?" He snatched a last handful of sticky almonds.

"Medieval England didn't offer indoor air-conditioned arenas." She grabbed a few nuts from his cone. "Are you expecting an indoor movie theater with reclining stadium seats?"

"Does that mean no?"

Her shoulders shook with mirth. "An unequivocal no."

As they wandered, munched, and sipped cold drinks, her gaze riveted to a display of handmade jewelry, and she lingered to rhapsodize over a cross pendant suspended from a gold chain. The artisan ran his fingers along the smokey quartz beads, zeroing in on the center green stone.

"Pearls and peridot." He brought the necklace closer so Ashley could examine the quality and craftsmanship. "These necklaces are one of a kind. A set of matching earrings is also available."

"The cross is gorgeous and the design so intricate." She turned it over to view the price tag and pushed it back toward him. "Unfortunately, it's way out of my price range."

David bent and kissed her cheek. "Do you like the necklace?"

"I love it."

"Then it's yours."

She placed her hand on his, her smile shy. "I could never accept such an expensive gift."

"You'd deprive me from buying a special necklace for my fairest lady?"

Before she objected further, he settled up with the vendor

and hooked the fine gold chain around her neck. She fingered the cross and grinned into the hand mirror the vendor supplied.

"You're too generous." She kissed David with so much enthusiasm he considered purchasing the entire jewelry display.

"My pleasure." He tripped on the words, his throat welling with emotion.

He was starting to care for her more than he ever dreamed possible.

A rosy tint enhanced her fine cheekbones. "I realize a Renaissance Faire isn't your favorite way to spend the day."

He cradled her, kissed her again. "I'm enjoying every single minute more than I ever imagined." To his astonishment, this was the most pleasant afternoon he ever recalled.

She changed direction, evidently distracted by the scent of leather at a table touting handcrafted leather goods. He grabbed the opportunity to purchase the matching earrings to Ashley's necklace and slipped the gift bag into his shorts pocket.

He pointed to a ride, a swinging suspended barrel. Thrilled screams from the riders blasted whenever the barrel flew into the air. "Are you agreeable to riding the Barrel of Mayhem?"

"Absolutely. It looks a little tamer than the Whirl and Hurl." She set her hand on his outstretched palm. "Human-powered, naturally."

He had turned to a booth to purchase tickets for the ride when a vendor at Robin Hood Archery called out, "How are your abilities with a bow and arrow, sir? Step right up and win your lovely lady a simulated diamond ring. All you have to do is strike the tree stump. If you hit the target six times in a row, you'll win her a cuddly black bear."

David stepped to the booth and scrutinized the bows

and arrows laid out on a table. He knew nothing about archery, but how hard could the sport be? No special equipment was required, and his one good eye boasted perfect vision.

Decisively, he dug in his pocket for loose dollar bills.

The vendor focused on David. "All it takes is a steady hand, flexible muscles, and a cool disposition."

Ashley giggled. "David, the man must know you."

He scanned the selection, the sleek curves of the bows, and decided on a recurved design.

Ashley tapped him on the shoulder. "I thought we were riding Mayhem?"

He steered her around and yanked off his metal mesh hood. "Not when I'm presented with the prospect of winning you a diamond ring. The opportunity is practically falling in my lap."

"Only takes one bulls-eye." The vendor's voice lowered as he peered at David. "Haven't I seen you somewhere? You look like that hermit artist guy. My wife showed me a picture in a magazine last year of a famous painting, *Lady by the River*. The article reported you were taking the art world by storm."

A sidelong grin accompanied David's attempt to correct the vendor. "*Woman by the River*."

"Huh?"

"*Woman by the River*," David repeated. "Not lady."

The vendor waved a hand. "Woman, lady, something like that."

Ashley met David's grin with a challenging smile. "You realize that no one can find the actual river in your painting."

"My wife said the same thing," the vendor agreed.

"You're kidding. The river is obvious." David shot a stunned look at them both, his eyes narrowing as he took in Ashley's vibrant expression.

Tension filled the air as David secured the arrow, stretched back the bow string, and took aim.

"Rembrandt!" Ashley shouted.

The arrow missed and landed in a mound of dirt.

He lowered the bow, tossed her an offended look, and picked another arrow.

"Not Rembrandt," the vendor corrected. "This hermit painter is supposed to be more avant-garde. My wife claims his paintings are fine art and innovative. Me? I'll take a Michelangelo any day."

While David pondered whether he'd just been complimented or insulted, he granted Ashley a self-assured smirk. He notched his arrow and tried again. On his last attempt, he'd finally gotten the hang of archery and hit the tree stump.

"Hurray! You've won your girlfriend a diamond ring." The vendor fumbled behind the display and planted a plastic case in David's outstretched palm.

David peeled off the cellophane and examined the cheap faux diamond.

"Will you wear my ring?" He gazed at Ashley, delighted by the brilliant smile crossing her face. "I'll buy you something better, something bigger. I promise."

"I don't need anything better." She extended her right hand. "The sentiment is what's meaningful."

He slipped the ring on her fourth finger. "Now it's official."

"What is?"

"We're formally dating." At the realization of how much the moment meant to him, he cleared his throat and noted a banner draped over a gigantic rocking horse. "Like the sign states, I'm a contented fairgoer. I hope you're contented too."

"I am. Thank you." She pressed the ring to her cheek as if it were the most precious item she'd ever worn. "David?"

"Hmm?"

Her lilting voice uttering his name had an odd effect. He felt alive and valued. He trusted her, trusted her enough to be his true self. He felt safe, encouraged by the knowledge he'd found the woman of his dreams.

Here. Not in Manhattan, not at a fancy art gallery in Los Angeles, or on a swanky island in the Caribbean. Here. In this tiny Southern community, that embraced their faith in God.

He smiled as he stuffed the knight's hood into a free pocket.

He was still smiling when they passed a line-up of food stands that led to the jousting arena. At the entrance, he deliberated about ordering an enormous turkey leg and muttered, "A carnivore's dream."

He scanned the gigantic field, humming with merchants, scampering youngsters, and a horde of men clothed in tunics, capes, and plumed feather hats.

Ashley gazed at the scene and sighed. "Sadly, there are no chocolate candy bars sold during the Renaissance, either."

"You eased your sugar fix when you devoured the choco-late-covered almonds."

A frown formed between her delicately arched eyebrows. "You ate half of them."

"Me? Two handfuls at the most."

Good-naturedly, she swatted his forearm. "Your handfuls were more like scoops. The jousting is starting. I don't want to miss it."

"David Fodero!" a familiar male voice called.

David and Ashley turned.

Julian Wilson and his wife, Nora, stood by the fish and chips stand. Julian sported a high-collared hourglass-fit jacket, white ruffled shirt, and matching breeches, every inch the country gentleman. Nora raised a monocle to her eye and waved. She wore a linen sheath and buttercups were braided in her hair.

David looked around. He and Ashley were hopelessly trapped between a mob and a musician playing the hammered dulcimer.

In the spirit of friendship, Nora extended her hands as she and Julian approached. "How fun to see you two here."

David inclined his head. "What a coincidence."

Julian surveyed David's costume and chuckled. "You're a knight, I gather?"

"I'm a knight if you're a country gentleman."

"Touché."

"I hoped no one would see me except Ashley." David reached for her hand. "I have a reputation to preserve."

"Don't we all." Ever the diplomat, Julian sidetracked the exchange. "Before you ask, Pickle is safe with Samantha. Your dog and ours get along grand."

"Excellent." David had asked Samantha if she could watch his dog, and she'd cheerfully agreed.

"Pickle is so well-behaved, I'll dog-sit whenever I'm free, Mr. Fodero," she'd assured him.

"Did Samantha tell you where Ashley and I were headed?" David inquired.

Julian's smile was one of exaggerated innocence. "As a matter of fact, she did."

"Are you two planning to watch the jousting match?" Nora asked. "We can sit together." With an exclamation of delight, she stared at Ashley's necklace. "Oh my. How lovely!"

Ashley stole a glance at David beneath her long lashes. "David bought it for me at an artisan shop."

"Gorgeous. And your ring." Nora gazed meaningfully at Ashley's right hand. A slow, disbelieving smile bloomed. "Is it new also?"

"David won it for me at the archery game." Ashley tossed her shiny hair over her shoulders. "We're officially dating."

Nora's perceptive eyes met Ashley's. "Congratulations!"

"You're a lucky man." Julian offered his usual clap on David's back. "Aren't you going to kiss her?"

David appraised Ashley's exquisite features. "I believe another kiss is in order."

She displayed a jaunty smile. "Is it?"

"Absolutely." His husky voice betrayed his affection. His lips moved closer, and he kissed her long and thoroughly.

"Remember, our generous Lord will give each of us another day," Julian interrupted.

As the couples picked up their steps to stay with the crowd, Julian joked with David about whether the archery game was fixed, especially when Ashley recapped the vendor's announcement that David had six tries.

David tucked Ashley's fingers in the crook of his arm. "I made a bulls-eye on my last shot."

She flicked a glance at her right hand. "If you had hit the stump all six times, you would've won me a cuddly black bear."

"Which do you prefer? The ring or the bear?"

"The ring."

Her expressive eyes shone with a love he recognized because he felt it, too. The exhilarating promise of a future together beckoned. Ashley was faultless in every sense— goodness, generosity, and a devout faith he felt growing inside himself. A warmth of happiness flowed through him.

The foursome made their way into the arena. In seconds, the space was split with thunderous applause as a juggler appeared near the tent opening.

"It's a shame Ashley is leaving on Saturday." Nora started for a row of empty seats. "Luckily, Greenwood isn't that far away. A little less than two hours, right?"

David grasped Ashley's hand to help her climb the metal steps. "You live in Greenwood?"

She looked at him as if he were unjustly vilifying her. "Yes. Why?"

"We've seen each all week, and I never asked where you lived." His mind raced. "I'm familiar with the town. Do you know a woman named Nancy Trainor? She owns an art gallery there."

"My art studio is connected to her gallery, along with a café."

He stilled. Thoughts came rushing at him, too numerous to comprehend.

Ashley had looked familiar the first day they'd met at his cabin.

As the jousting commenced, the knights paraded out of the tent waving red and blue flags, their magnificent, broad-chested horses flaunting a bard, a glitzy cloth that displayed the knight's emblem. They were introduced and presented to the audience amidst good-natured cheers and boos. A drum roll began, and demonstrations of the knights' skills on horseback ensued as they knocked over progressively smaller targets with their wooden lances.

The announcer lauded unbridled participation, which prompted Julian and Nora to stand and clap. The crowd dissolved in laughter as a jester appeared and cartwheeled across the ground.

David became increasingly aware of the beautiful woman seated next to him, her posture rigid. She didn't stand. She didn't clap. She didn't move. The diamond captured the sun's rays and gleamed.

"Points are awarded for broken lances." Julian pointed to a knight standing by his horse. "No points awarded for broken shields."

What about a broken heart? Any points awarded for that?

Julian and Nora seemed completely unaware of David's rising tension or Ashley's silence. The rallying roar increased as the knights charged and battled.

For the next fifteen minutes, Nora kept up an animated conversation with Ashley, while Ashley responded in monosyllables.

David carefully considered Ashley's lovely profile. The beaded cross swayed when she shifted.

And during that time, he pondered.

Finally, it dawned on him. She knew he couldn't see out of his right eye and had purposefully moved to his left. In fact, she always did that.

In addition, whenever she rode in his truck, she always sat up straight and turned toward him when she spoke.

She was empathetic and cared about him. She was considerate, often reassuring and loving. *Yes, loving.*

Or so he imagined.

As the jousting continued, his speculations took him further, his recollections in turmoil.

When she'd shown up at his cabin, on a road with no outlet, she'd claimed her convertible had broken down. Once she stepped inside, she spent several minutes fawning over his canvas.

Her friend Sarah had come to the rescue and "fixed" her car.

On another day, Ashley had gifted him with a basket of peaches she'd placed in his cabin, admitting she'd snooped inside. Then she'd appeared at his favorite spot where he painted.

All these coincidences? Maybe. Maybe not.

He shook his head. An idiot could've figured it out sooner. Ashley's studio was linked to the art gallery carrying his paintings, which was the reason why she'd looked so familiar. When he'd visited Nancy several months ago to drop off a painting, he'd glimpsed Ashley on the floor of her studio with a student. She'd smiled and waved.

Nancy must have sent Ashley to Cherish to figure out why he hadn't responded to her messages.

He'd trusted that meeting Ashley in Cherish was circumstantial. Fate. In actuality, it had been planned and calculated. She'd come to Cherish to spy on him.

But why?

He gave a short, bitter laugh, and Ashley glanced at him. He looked away.

Because of money. The stream of revenue from his paintings was obviously an asset for Nancy and the other shop owners.

Ashley wasn't interested in him for himself.

With that knowledge, something inside him splintered apart.

What else had Ashley conveniently forgotten? The fact she was Nancy's spy? The fact she used him, his art, to fill her coffers? All three businesses—the gallery, the café, and Ashley's studio—relied on each other's sales to survive. Nancy had mentioned that to him when he'd commented on the businesses' adjoining doors. Customers walked from one shop to another.

He pondered all this, though, but said nothing. No matter how he tried, he couldn't focus on the match or Julian's jesting commentary.

When the joust finished after an endless sixty minutes, he curtly declined Julian's invitation to watch a glass blower, drawing the other man's piercing gaze. David used Pickle's long day with Samantha as an excuse.

After he and Ashley exchanged their costumes for street clothes, the drive to Cherish was hushed and oppressive.

Sitting in the passenger seat, Ashley tentatively asked, "Is anything wrong?"

"Wrong?" His knuckles tightened on the steering wheel.

She sat straighter. An eternity passed before he realized she was waiting for him to speak.

As they made the final turnoff, he followed the road up a hill, straight as an arrow. He pulled into a lookout point and shut off the engine.

"Ashley Madden." He stared out the window into the fog-shrouded valley. "Who are you?"

"I'm Ashley."

"We've concluded you're not a mountain climber."

"I confessed."

"And you poked around my cabin when you delivered the peaches."

"I confessed to that too."

"You're a Christian woman?"

Her gaze raised to his, glittering with tears. "I try my best."

He swallowed, tasting a heartbreaking defeat. "Maybe your best isn't good enough."

She groped for a handkerchief in her purse and dabbed at her eyes. "If you're concerned about my art studio being located in Greenwood—"

"This has nothing to do with Greenwood." Already, he felt himself separating from her. "I'm trying to deal with your deception."

"I'm not following."

"Aren't you?" A kaleidoscope of distrust emerged. "You should've been up front with me from the beginning. Told me why you landed in Cherish and what you expected to find out."

"David, I didn't intend to deceive you. It's just that you never responded to Nancy's emails and texts and—"

"Let me guess. She was worried."

Her lips trembled. "We all were."

"Worried about me? Or were you concerned about the

revenue loss if Nancy wasn't able to secure any more of my paintings? What am I to you, a dollar sign?"

"What am I to you, an excuse to procrastinate?"

"Don't be ridiculous."

A mix of distressing emotions crossed her face. "Likewise."

"You drove fifty miles to Cherish and planned on spending the weekend nosing around. How did you find me?"

"Sarah suggested I contact the state park ranger."

"She was in on this deception too."

"Yes, but—" Ashley tore her gaze from his. "The ranger gave me the name of your road. It was the easiest way to track you down."

"I assume you've reported the news of my eyesight loss to Nancy." David gathered steam to deliver his ace advantage. "Well, tell her this. I'll sell no more paintings in her gallery."

If he ever actually painted again.

Ashley didn't respond at first. Instead, she rested a hand on his arm. "I'm sorry. There were many instances when I—" Tears formed at the corner of her eyes. "I've loved every moment we're together and never wanted to spoil it."

Love. The word brought hope and sadness, snapping his self-control.

"No more of those, I assure you."

"No more of what?"

"We won't spend any more time together." He leaned his head against the seat. In the empty space between them, the distance grew wider. "I'm returning to New York."

"To paint?"

"I'm unsure of my abilities, my career." He rolled down the window. The wind carried the noise of the town below. Cherish. Once, he hoped to belong there. Not anymore.

"You're dealing with your loss the wrong way." Raggedly,

she inhaled. She still had her hand on his forearm. "Keep painting. You can overcome this, the way Sarah did when she confronted her deafness. Her life is full and happy. Rely on God's promise."

"Which is what?"

"God will walk with you through the storm."

He shrugged off her hand. He couldn't forgive deceit. He couldn't forgive God for placing an unfair hardship on him. He'd never forgiven his father. Ashley only proved what David already recognized. Few people could be trusted. Certainly not her.

His motions quick and jerky, he started the engine, rolled up the window, and switched on the air-conditioning. The truck idled. "You're attempting to convert me back to Christianity after learning my religious views?"

"I've always wanted to help you." The tension in her exquisite face gave way to pleading. "Through God's grace, my specialty is fixing problems."

"I'm not a broken car."

"So what if you have a handicap? Don't deny it. Embrace it. Never give up. You're commissioned to paint a portrait of a special church. Memorial Street Church is a building, but the real church is what happens on the inside."

"It's over Ashley." He couldn't trust his voice to say more. To consider the magnificent future he'd once envisioned for them.

"I understand." Ashley didn't falter for a beat. "Now understand this. God will always be there for you."

"What part of *church not being part of my life* don't you comprehend?"

"If there's anything I can do—"

"There isn't." He enunciated the words clearly.

"David, I'm sorry."

"We've already invested a conversation around your apologies. No need for another."

For the remainder of the drive to town, stillness reigned.

As they neared the inn, he slowed, then parked near the curb. "Go home, Ashley. Go back to Greenwood and take the art supplies I bought with you."

She raised her chin. Her face reddened. "You're joking, right? Keep your supplies." Her fingers fumbled with the chain as she unhooked the necklace. "Take this." She placed the necklace on the seat. Her hands shook as she removed the ring and flung it at him. "And don't forget this."

"Those were gifts." He ducked as the ring hit the window. "They're for you."

"I don't want them!" Her shoulders set. Her glorious eyes glittered with unshed tears. She shoved open the door before he could go around and open it.

She stomped from the truck and didn't turn around.

He watched her leave, fighting with himself, wanting to dash after her, but stopping himself from looking more like a fool than he already was. As she flew up the steps and entered the inn, his stomach sank. Somewhere inside, he knew his happiness was slipping away.

He should reach out and grab it. Take the initiative. Life is short.

No. Mission accomplished. He'd broken off their relationship.

It was for the best. They lived miles apart. Long-distance dating seldom worked.

Doubt simmered inside him as he picked up the ring and arranged the necklace with the earrings. He hesitated. He'd placed the ring on her finger. She'd pressed the ring to her cheek as if it were her most precious possession, then kissed him with unabandoned joy.

A faux diamond ring that meant so much.

He stared at the inn in silence. He needed to come to grips with his decision.

The day had held such promise. And just like that, happiness was gone.

Sighing, he briefly closed his eyes. No practical man heeded his heart first. And he was a practical man.

He debated one last time, facing the future without her in his life.

Then he shifted his truck into gear and headed for the Wilsons' home to pick up Pickle.

CHAPTER 14

Some painters transform the sun into a yellow spot, others
transform the yellow spot into the sun.
- Picasso

*A*fter a restless night, Ashley got out of bed, groggy from fragmentary dreams. She showered, phoned Sarah and left a voice message that she was leaving, then quickly packed her suitcase. The forecast predicted an unseasonably cool day, and she dressed in tan cotton slacks, a blue blouse, and a jeans jacket.

She descended the inn's broad staircase on rubbery legs and scanned the lobby. The pendulum clock rang out the early hour. The clink of silver coming from the solarium meant breakfast was ready to be served.

Julian stood at the reception desk and hailed her with a chipper "Greetings."

She approached with her suitcase in tow. "I'm checking out today."

He frowned. "I thought you were staying longer."

"No. I'm done here." She wiped an errant tear. "Naturally, I'm happy to pay for the extra nights I reserved."

"There are folks on a waiting list, and your room is easy to fill." As soon as he finished processing her refund, he said, "None of my business, but I assume things didn't work out with David?"

"That's a kind spin."

"You both fairly floated in and out of here. I remarked to Nora that you two have a chemistry people rarely share."

Ashley managed a wan smile. "Did we?"

"You're lucky."

"Coincidental. Circumstance." She shook her head in denial. "We had a falling out, and it was my fault. I apologized."

"Did he accept your apology?"

"Hardly." She pushed up the sleeves of her jacket. "Just the opposite."

"Hopefully you gave him something to think about."

Her face heated. *Yes, had she ever.*

On the mountainous return drive to Greenwood, Ashley blamed herself for handling things so badly. She had an explanation for David on the tip of her tongue more often than not, but in the end, she'd lacked courage. David clearly cared for her. He'd placed her on a pedestal she hadn't deserved.

"Your sincerity is disarming." He'd sealed his declaration with a kiss.

Stunned by her leaking tears, she pulled her convertible over to the side of the road. She'd been hurt before, her heart broken, but never like this.

She recalled his high-handed dismissal. David, the handsome, impossible artist with a sterling character. David, the man she'd come to love.

178

No. It wasn't possible to fall in love in only a few days. For a second time, she'd been charmed by a man who feigned interest. He probably had already found another woman more to his liking. Sophisticated and alluring and ravishing.

She forced herself to breathe while her heart hammered a heavy beat. There was no sense in denying her emotions. She missed his lazy smile, his wry humor.

She reached for her phone. Perhaps she could text him and apologize again. Her pride would be salvaged if he accepted her apology, even if he was coolly unenthusiastic.

Julian had offered insight into the chemistry between her and David, and she'd denied it. Sadly, her denial wasn't true.

There was interest and magic. Judging by his smiles, David had enjoyed being with her. The memory of his warm lips moving on hers, his murmurings. *"You're beautiful, Ashley."*

Her, the plainest of plain Janes.

Her heart swelled as other memories surfaced.

The first time they officially met at his cabin. Their pillow fight.

The afternoon he declared he was painting *her*, and how she imagined their laughter could be heard for miles.

He cared deeply, which was why he was so hurt by her deception. He'd assumed she cared for him, and then concluded she was after his money.

She slumped in her seat. If he only realized how much she *did* care.

However, he was gone now. Gone forever.

A lump of sadness swelled in her throat, but she vowed not to cry anymore. Unwanted tears trickled, and she brushed them away.

"Show me the way, Lord." She closed her eyes and prayed. "I'm your daughter. You are my friend. I'm sorry for hurting David. I can't control the guilt welling up inside me because of my wrongdoing. I'll rely on your healing grace."

She switched on the ignition and turned the radio to a contemporary Christian station. This drive would mark her last trip from Cherish.

A DAY LATER, in response to Nancy's queries, Ashley explained David's eyesight loss.

"Will he continue to paint?" Worried shadows underscored Nancy's brown eyes when she'd swept into Ashley's studio and claimed the nearest chair. "I—we, all three of our businesses, need his pieces to survive."

"He refused. I pray he will concentrate on healing and taking care of himself."

Nancy took an overlong time, adjusting her flowing bohemian skirt. "Are you suggesting he can't paint?"

"He *won't* paint, at least not to sell any pieces in your gallery."

Ashley turned to the sound of commotion. Two children in wheelchairs argued over the same brush. She lifted one of the children's wrists, then the other, and clapped their hands together simultaneously. Once they giggled, she encouraged their friendship and asked them to share. Then she swiveled to Nancy.

"Honestly, David can see. For him, it's a struggle to accept his disability."

Nancy stood, staring critically at Ashley. "You look terrible, by the way."

Ashley was fully aware her complexion was pale, and that lines of sadness marked her mouth. Wryly, she replied, "Thanks."

"When you extended your stay in Cherish, I assumed you were having a blast."

"Cherish has a storybook quality, and the residents are right-minded and decent." Unwilling to show her regret and heartbreak, Ashley pleaded busyness and excused herself to tend to a curly-haired girl who demanded attention. "I'm grateful to be back."

"*My relationships never go over three months,*" David had told her.

He'd certainly succeeded this time.

THE NEXT MONTH drifted by in a haze of desolation. Ashley continuously checked her phone, hoping to hear from David. Perhaps a text.

Nothing.

Too many times every day, she attempted to shake off the heartbreaking memories that haunted her.

David playing fetch with his dog.

David absorbed in taking photographs of a tree, of a river. David photographing her.

She immersed herself in teaching her precious pupils. When a David Fodero painting was alluded to during a meeting with students and their parents, Ashley couldn't respond. Hiding her face from her students' puzzled glances, she rushed from the studio and into Nancy's gallery, tears streaming down her cheeks.

"What happened?" Nancy grasped Ashley's cold hands.

"David and I were together every day. He was wonderful."

Nancy's fingers tightened. "Will you please tell me more?"

Ashley bent her head. "I deceived him, although it wasn't intentional. I was a coward and never explained my reason for being in Cherish. When he discovered my deception, he was angry."

"You're not deceitful, Ashley. Praying helps. God's got this."

Ashley stared at the blank wall where Nancy had repeatedly hung David's paintings. Once again, she was alone. Once again, she relied on herself and her faith in God.

WHEN THE CALENDAR neared the end of July, Nancy casually mentioned that David had moved back to his penthouse in Manhattan. He'd phoned to inform her he was selling his cabin, and felt he owed her some explanation for his whereabouts because they were old friends.

"If anyone wants to buy the cabin, direct them to my agent in New York," he'd instructed.

Ashley had been thanking a sturdy five-year-old who'd offered her a puffy white hydrangea flower.

Her head jerked up when Nancy relayed the news. She rubbed her palms on her plaid shorts and turned to the half-dozen children staring at her.

"What fun we're going to have today," she declared. "Has anyone ever painted a picture of a tree?"

Smiling at the children's eager, enthusiastic faces, she threw herself into their paint splattering and chortles, giving scrupulous attention to each and every brushstroke.

ON THE FIRST Saturday of August, David stood in the living room of his Manhattan apartment, scrutinizing the painting perched on his easel. He'd painted Ashley, sitting at the top of an oak tree, surrounded by wildflowers—fiery pinks, cardinal reds, and gray-purple violets.

His depiction of her was delicate, resembling a fairy—mischievous and kind, the size of a thumb. He'd captured her profile—small turned-up nose and rounded chin. The luxuriant mass of honey-blond hair, the full pink lips, the cream-colored complexion. He'd harbored the hope she'd someday see it.

Torn between his internal critic and the lovely portrait, he gave a grim laugh. He only needed to make a few additions beginning with a river ... somewhere.

He'd arrived in Manhattan, believing the anonymity of the city would ease the sadness in his gut. He'd painted for hours with an uncontained fervor. Now he stood back and assessed the painting he'd begun in Cherish.

"What's your opinion, Pickle?" He observed his dog snoring by the window. "Ashley is beautiful, isn't she?"

Yes, she was. Only he hadn't captured her genuine beauty, the kindness radiating from her heart.

He stayed where he was, lost in thought.

When he'd retreated to his cabin the day of the Renaissance Faire, he'd devoted himself to his work for weeks. In all that time, he'd produced a few lithographs and sketches, and nearly completed the commissioned painting of Memorial Street Church.

He had never missed a deadline, and the painting was scheduled to be delivered to Marge Addyson by the final week in August. He'd left it in Cherish, assuming he'd add final touches when he returned to pack the last of his boxes.

He'd decided on a two-sided art, two renderings, past and present, of the same church. He'd sketched the older version in charcoal, as he'd mentioned to Ashley. He'd enhanced the painting of the present-day church with a sparkly purple star in the corner and his initials, *D.F.*

Beneath was one letter.

A.

The letter and the star were minuscule.

He hadn't been able to help himself. His dreams were of her. Always of her.

The expansive window of his penthouse faced Central

Park, and rain pounded on the glass. It had rained constantly. Incessant and never-ending, and he'd come to realize he vastly preferred sunshine.

He stared out at the relentless raindrops, the wet pavement far below, pedestrians walking swiftly and carrying umbrellas.

He caught his reflection. His forehead creased with fatigue, and he averted his gaze. He couldn't look at himself anymore. Self-doubt had become his foremost companion.

He sank down on the enormous leather sofa and placed his head in his hands. He hadn't trusted his father after learning of his unfaithfulness. He'd never forgiven him.

David opened the Bible he'd purchased when he'd landed in New York. He leafed to Psalms, reflecting on the passage about God's grace and forgiveness. His mercy was great.

He turned the Bible over, running his thumb along the edges of the sacred book.

David longed to put the past behind him and proceed. But how could he do that when his hopes had abandoned him? Or rather, he'd abandoned his dreams. If people realized his backstory, they'd sympathize. He'd never had any prior health problems. Why an eyesight loss?

Rewind. Remember the exhilarating days with Ashley. The happiest moments of his life had been the hours spent with her.

He'd convinced himself she'd played him for a fool. But hadn't she declared her love for him? Not outright, but in numerous instances.

He straddled two conflicting visions of his future. Him alone in his Manhattan studio, endless months painting in solitude. Or days in Cherish, accompanied by the gorgeous Ashley Madden. Her fresh scent of lemon and sage, wholesome and uplifting, so different from the expensive perfumes of the women he'd escorted to fancy parties.

He could still feel Ashley in his arms, her hand touching his heart. Her gaze had darkened with empathy when he talked about his father.

And there were other times. Pleasurable, joyous times.

Ashley, sitting in a tree:

"I'm an adult, but it doesn't mean I should give up everything I loved to do when I was young," she'd said. *"The view is different up here. Better."*

Better.

Ashley peering in his freezer.

"What kind of guy doesn't eat Hungry-Man dinners?"

Ashley jostling the vending machine:

"Grand idea," she'd said as she inserted his quarters. *"Sadly, it isn't working."*

She was right. Being apart wasn't the answer. He'd presumed self-worth came from his paintings, not himself. That his job defined his existence. The hardest lesson was facing his weakness. But weakness could be turned into strength.

He could paint. He could overcome his impairment by refusing to fixate on it. Instead, he could apply his efforts to helping others and truly appreciate the positive.

With Ashley.

Reach out. It was worth it.

They deserved to be happy.

He recalled the sermon he'd related to her, the sermon he'd heard as a child:

"The blessing ahead of you is bigger than any battle you left behind," the aged pastor had proclaimed.

Those words were appropriate for yesterday and today. David sent a belated acknowledgement to his long-ago pastor, and to his mother for dragging him to church.

"Lord, you must have a plan for me," he prayed. "Ashley

provided inspirational messages every time we were together, and I'm ready to connect the dots."

He came to his feet, his mind made up.

"I'm glad you're a top-notch passenger, Pickle." He scooped up his dog, already deciding to charter a plane to Atlanta, then a car to Cherish. "We're heading back to my cabin tomorrow. You'll sleep in the carry-on. Just think, you might soon get another belly rub from a certain beautiful woman you'll recognize."

David yanked out his phone, then paused. He tried to avoid thinking about his next obstacle, but here it was.

He didn't have the slightest inkling if Ashley would even speak to him. In all these weeks, he hadn't contacted her, hoping she'd contact him.

She hadn't. He hadn't. Two stubborn individuals.

All he knew was that he loved her, and he knew in his heart she loved him.

He wasn't certain of the reaction he'd receive or if she'd agree to his plan.

Never give up.

He was eager to see her. Eager to make things right.

He plugged in the number for an esteemed Manhattan jeweler and requested an early morning appointment. The business didn't open until ten, but for the exorbitant price David was willing to pay, he was confident the jeweler would meet him earlier.

"Tomorrow," David said to Pickle as he set him down in his doggie bed. "We're going home."

CHAPTER 15

Action is the foundational key to all success.
- Picasso

"David Fodero." Nancy Trainor's eyes narrowed as David strode into the Greenwood art gallery carrying an art portfolio case. "I never expected to see you again."

He grinned. "Yet here I am."

"Is that a painting for my gallery?" She zeroed in on the case, and the withering look on her face died. "Can I sell whatever is in there?"

"Sorry." He broke off, nodding casually to the art patrons. "It's not for sale."

People gasped and discreetly gestured toward him. A noticeable silence ensued.

He heard his name whispered but didn't turn. Instead, he quickened his steps and followed the sounds of giggling children behind an adjoining closed door.

He spotted Ashley sitting cross-legged on her studio floor before the door fully shut. She wore a pair of jean shorts and a fitted purple T-shirt. Her hair was secured in a high ponytail.

The room was tidy, and white canvases lay in a pile, along with paper towels. A dizzying array of artwork hung on the wall. A handwashing station was tucked in one corner, and the smell of acrylic paint filled the air.

Surrounded by a group of children wearing imaginative orange smocks, she smiled at a slim little boy dipping his brush in a jar of water.

"Freddie, try to concentrate." Ashley snatched a clean brush from a metal bucket. "Trees aren't hard to draw."

David stepped nearer. His heart hammered in hope, in anticipation.

"Because anyone can paint a tree," he said softly.

Two boys in wheelchairs looked up at him and gaped.

Ashley jumped to her feet. Her fine, pale eyebrows drew together. Her hand touched her throat. "David?"

"Hey, I recognize you." One of the boys wheeled his chair protectively in front of Ashley. His thin shoulders squared. "You're the artist guy Miss Ashley cried about when my mother mentioned your name a few weeks ago."

"I'm here to tell her I'm sorry." David set down the case. His gaze remained on Ashley. Her face lost all color as she continued to stare at him. "I hope she'll forgive me for being a fool."

Tears poured down her cheeks as she picked her way between the children and flew into David's outstretched arms.

"She's crying again," the second boy in a wheelchair remarked accusingly.

"I'm fine." Ashley's shoulders shook with sobbing. "I'm crying tears of joy."

David framed her face and wiped her cheeks with his thumbs. He sheltered her from the children's gazes. "I missed you. I came to tell you I love you."

She slid her hands around his neck. "I love you too."

"Okay, you two." Nancy stepped into the room, unsuccessfully hiding her amusement behind a mask of genteel professionalism. She looked at the children. "Miss Ashley has a substitute teacher filling in for her."

"Who?" The boys chimed.

"Me."

David smiled his appreciation at the keenly perceptive Nancy. She diverted the children by debating color combinations and an abbreviated embellishment of the tree the one boy had begun to paint.

David steered Ashley to a secluded corner. "I couldn't stay away." He kissed her forehead, his fingers drifting up and down her spine. "Please forgive me."

"I'm the one who needs forgiving."

"No." He shook his head, his laugh bitter. "I focused on myself, my pride. In so doing, I overlooked what's most important."

"David, don't feel guilty."

"I have several reasons for being here, but guilt isn't primary."

"What is then?"

"I want to have sons and daughters with hazel eyes and a tender, giving heart. I want to give you my name and all that I have."

She bit back a smile.

He withdrew a jewelry case from his pocket and handed it to her. "Ashley Madden, will you marry me?"

Elation shimmered in her eyes as she opened the case. The ring was larger than the imitation ring he'd won at the Renaissance Faire. This diamond was four carats and exquisitely cut, reflecting the natural light of the sunshine streaming through the window.

"Yes. I'll marry you." Her gaze radiated with love. "Meeting you was a gift from God."

He had hoped she'd recognized the extraordinary hand of fate that had led them to each other. There were no coincidences. He'd met an angel who believed in him and loved him.

He slipped the ring onto the fourth finger of her left hand and kissed her palm. "We're officially engaged."

"You are?" Nancy peered up from the center of a circle surrounded by children. "I didn't mean to eavesdrop but—"

"What's that?" The slight boy named Freddie examined David's carry case. "Aren't you going to show us what's inside?" Freddie inched nearer as the other children gathered round.

"It's a special painting." David reached for Ashley's hand. Her smile radiated with love, and he was certain he'd gotten his first glimpse of heaven.

From the second she'd accepted his hand; he'd recognized the special bond between them. Carefully, because he didn't want to break their connection, he continued, "The decision is totally up to Miss Ashley."

"Why, Mr. Fodero? It's not her painting." Freddie waited for the other children to join him and echo his opinion. "The painting is yours."

"I painted the canvas, but the subject is essential." David focused on Ashley.

She smiled. "Go ahead."

"Yay!" For several seconds, the room filled with laughter from seven children and Nancy, all sharing a collective goal: discovering what was inside David's carrying case.

He pulled the canvas from the case amidst a variety of oohs and ahhs.

"That's Miss Ashley!" Freddie pointed to a whimsical woman sitting in an oak tree. "She's so pretty. Why is she up there?"

"She likes to climb trees," David replied.

Flowers of every color and type surrounded her—gold, silver, and dots of colorful wildflowers. Pickle snoozed beside the tree.

Ashley turned to him. "Where is Pickle today?"

"I left him with Samantha Wilson. When I arrived from New York, I rented a jeep, and drove several treacherous curves on the road connecting Greenwood to Cherish."

She laughed. "The route is challenging."

"Fortunately, it isn't as difficult as climbing Grandfather Mountain."

She took a step back. "Have you ever climbed—?

"Never."

"David, you titled your work," Nancy interrupted, examining the words written at the top of the painting.

Freddie tugged at the bell-shaped sleeve of Nancy's blouse. "What does it say?"

"Mr. Fordero's initials, the letter A, and a sparkly purple star. The painting is titled *My Wife by the River*. My *wife*." Nancy's thick black eyebrows lifted in surprise, though she quickly recovered her diplomatic self. "Congratulations. You took a chance, there, David, didn't you?"

"I prayed."

"Your painting is superb."

"Thank you." He considered the words he'd wanted to write on the canvas.

My dearest Ashley. I vow to fill our days with faith and laughter. Please love me as much as I love you.

He feasted his eyes on her exquisite face. She had the ability to enchant and charm him. "Do you like it, Twinkle?"

"I can't trust my voice." The love in her fathomless hazel

eyes warmed his heart. "Thankfully, you attached my nose to my face."

He laughed. "Where else would I put it?"

"On the tree, on a cloud, floating somewhere in the sky."

"Mr. Fodero?" Freddie was scrutinizing the painting.

"Hmm?"

"Where's the river?"

Stunned, David sobered. "Can't you find it?"

"No." Freddie, along with Nancy and Ashley, murmured agreement.

"Mr. Fodero?"

David shifted. "Yes, Freddie?"

"What's the pointy gold thing growing out of the grass?"

Unable to suppress his amusement, David pulled Ashley nearer and kissed her hair. "Miss Ashley's cowlick."

EPILOGUE

 ne Year Later

"Ashley, we won't be able to do much more of this." David gazed at his beautiful wife, precariously balanced on a tree branch beside him.

"Why not?" Ashley popped a frozen chocolate cookie into her mouth and chewed. "The obstetrician advised sweets in moderation and claimed they're safe for the baby."

"I'm not referring to cookies." He gazed out at the lawn, the garden overflowing with zucchini. *What would they do with all that zucchini? Was there such a thing as zucchini bread?* "I'm discussing your penchant for climbing trees and dragging me up here alongside you."

"You won't let me climb alone anymore."

He patted her stomach. "With excellent reason, considering you're two months pregnant."

"Thank you for getting over your fear of tree climbing."

He chuckled. "I didn't have a choice. My heart was in my throat at the thought of you climbing up here alone."

She planted a sweet kiss on his lips, immediately appeasing him.

From below, Pickle romped across the lawn carrying a Frisbee, Ashley's mixed breed chihuahua racing at his heels. She'd adopted the five-pound dog with solid red fur and an angelic face from an animal rescue center in Greenwood, before relocating to Cherish. David affectionately named the puppy Dogzilla because of his feisty personality.

"Next month when I see the doctor, we should be able to hear the baby's heartbeat."

"I can't wait," he said in a husky voice he hardly recognized. "Together, my beautiful wife, we are complete."

He sipped his energy drink, then balanced it gingerly on a tray secured to a sturdy branch. He was trying to quit caffeine altogether and had weaned himself down to only one drink per day, which he savored.

He gazed at the Just Married sign they'd attached to his pickup a year earlier, for they'd gotten married not long after their engagement. He didn't own a vintage turquoise convertible. Instead, he'd opted for the sign embossed in bold turquoise letters. The sign now hung as a banner draped over the railing of his front porch. A reminder of a wonderful life, an exquisite marriage.

He'd wanted to give Ashley a lavish wedding in New York City with hundreds of guests, an orchestra providing entertainment, and a honeymoon in the Caribbean. She'd declined, requesting an intimate wedding and a quiet cabin in the Carolina mountains.

Two nights before their wedding, he'd sensed something was on her mind.

"I have one special request," she said, her smile dazzling.

She'd been typing last-minute notes on her laptop, and he adored her for handling all the pressure she'd been under so well—planning their wedding, moving to Cherish, and delivering a tearful goodbye to her students with a vow to visit often. Nancy had graciously offered to teach several classes, and Ashley's substitute teachers became full-time employees.

Before he had time to respond to her, a knock sounded on his cabin door. He opened it and stared at his two older brothers and his sister, Quinn. Ashley disappeared out the back door with Pickle and Dogzilla.

"Thanks for the piano books," Quinn began.

He hadn't heard from her since he'd sent the books, but Ashley had taught him about God's love and forgiveness. His doubts could die so that his faith could live.

"And congratulations on your wedding, David."

He shook hands with his brothers, embraced his sister, and invited them inside.

He hadn't imagined a way to forgive, especially when his eyesight loss still hung heavy on his mind. Ashley kept assuring him the hand of God was on his life.

On a sultry day at the end of August, he'd entered Memorial Street Church and presented Marge Addyson with the commissioned painting. Ashley had stood by his side. The first Sunday he'd attended church in over two decades, he had sung praises along to an amazing selection of worship music.

He had held Ashley's hand as they slid into a front pew and was encouraged by an inspiring sermon. All the while, he remembered her words: *Memorial Street Church is a building, but the real church is what happens on the inside.*

Since their engagement, and then marriage, he'd worked on a new collection of six avant-garde paintings, each with a theme centering on stars. The collection was scheduled to be exhibited at an exclusive auction house in New York. His return to the art world after nearly a year's absence assured widespread publicity and demand.

For now, he enveloped his wife in his arms.

"Thank you, David, for buying that empty lot in town," she said.

"It's not empty anymore. The art studio should be finished within the month."

"Special needs children and adults can enjoy the facilities." She smiled. "I love the name Starlight Vision."

He buried his face in her fragrant, lemon-scented hair. "Art should be nurtured. Creative expression and all that."

She laughed. "Typical artist."

"I hope every student, no matter their disability, will express themselves freely." He slid a hand around her waist, drawing her close. He kissed her stomach. "A miracle to cherish."

"Any plans after your art collection is sold?"

"I might consider purchasing a television for my study."

"You? The minimalist?" She didn't seem the least bit deceived by his nonchalance. "What will you watch? Another documentary?"

In between nuzzles, he murmured, "I'll begin with a certain black and white sitcom."

She began whistling the theme from *The Andy Griffith show*.

From high in a treetop, near a lushly designed cabin set in the woods, laughter rang out.

Pickle and Dogzilla barked and played tug-of-war with a plush striped elephant beneath a large oak tree.

Frozen cookies were left to thaw.

And all was right in a summer to cherish.

THE END

A NOTE FROM JOSIE

Dear Reader,

Thank you for reading my sweet inspirational romance, *A Summer To Cherish*. I hope you enjoyed this heartwarming story, featuring Ashley and David. This is the sixth book in my contemporary "Cherish" series.

Faith is fragile. Faith takes time. And the best solutions are always painted with love.

This story is set in the charming fictional small town of Cherish. Here, I introduce two new characters to our beloved mix of familiar heroes and heroines. I loved writing the spunky, fun heroine, and David was a swoon-worthy hero.

I also researched the hero's profession—painting—and his heartbreaking eyesight loss.

If you loved this story as much as I loved writing it, please help other people find it by posting your review.

A Summer To Cherish is available in ebook, paperback, Large Print paperback, audiobook, and Hardcover.

I'd love to meet you in person someday, but in the meantime, all I can offer is a sincere and grateful thank you. Without your support, my books would not be possible.

As I write my next sweet or inspirational romance, remember this: Have you ever tried something you were afraid to try because it mattered so much to you? I did, when I started writing. Take the chance, and just do something you love.

With sincere appreciation,

Josie Riviera

Love music?

My Spotify List for A Summer To Cherish is here.

Love the inspirational Cherish series? Be sure to grab all the books in the series here.

Or grab Cherished Hearts.

The entire series! 6 sweet, inspirational romances in 1 giant boxed set.

RECIPE FOR MELISSA'S SWEET & SOUR MEATBALLS

Ingredients:
   1 lb ground beef
   1 lb ground sausage
   Spices such as pepper, salt, garlic powder, onion powder
(whatever spices you enjoy in your meatballs)
   1 bottle of chili sauce
   1 large jar of orange marmalade

Directions:
   Mix ground beef, sausage, and spices to taste. Form small
meatballs, a little larger than a marble. Fry or bake meatballs
until almost cooked through. Set aside and drain.

In a Crock-Pot or large saucepan, mix the bottle of chili sauce and jar of marmalade. Over medium heat on the stove or high heat in the Crock-Pot, let the chili sauce and marmalade melt together. Once mixed, lower the heat and add the meatballs.

Mix the meatballs into the sauce. Allow to simmer for about 30 minutes. Lower the heat to keep warm.

Serve with toothpicks for guests to pick them up.

Or serve with rice or on a bun if wanting more of a dinner item.

Enjoy!

A LOVE SONG TO CHERISH
CHAPTER ONE PREVIEW

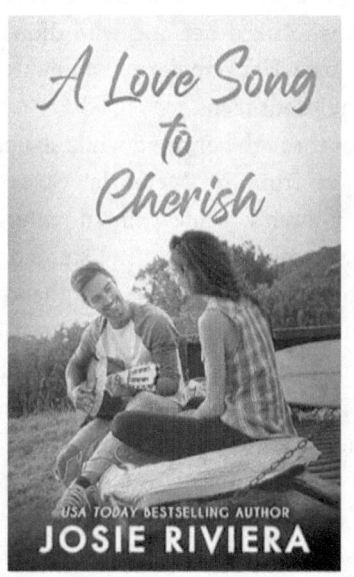

CHAPTER ONE

Dorothy Thompson had vowed to never set foot in Cherish, South Carolina, again. She didn't want to come back here.

She couldn't face it.

Sure, she'd lived in the tiny town all her life. And she'd felt alone, despite her popularity, her cheerleader friends, her football player boyfriend. Her mother had orchestrated Dorothy's status, keeping one eye on the stylish girls and the other eye on Dorothy.

"Everything will be perfect once you meet the right man, provided he's rich," her mother had explained. "A poor man does no more good than an eyeless needle."

Nonetheless, everything hadn't been perfect. Dorothy's wealthy boyfriend had cheated on her, and she couldn't compete with the stunning platinum blondes and redheads once she entered high school.

She'd told her mother she didn't care a cow-eatin' cabbage about who liked her and who didn't, although she knew it wasn't true. Her popularity had mattered very much during her tumultuous teens.

All this went through her mind while she parked her Ford Escort rental in front of Memorial Street Church. She regarded the church's white-painted exterior, the high-arched windows with their beautiful stained glass windows depicting scenes from the Bible and the ornately carved heavy wooden doors. Memories whispered of her singing beloved hymns in the church choir and Sunday school memorizing Bible verses in the church's basement.

So many memories for one little town.

She leaned her head against the driver's seat, no space in her mind for anything except sleep. The previous month, she'd endured the acute stage of opiate withdrawal along with the palpitations and tremors that came with it. And now Dr. Gantori, Dorothy's physician, had said the post-acute withdrawal stage could last two years.

She rubbed a hand over her puffy eyes. She was

exhausted, and no wonder. With a sigh, she reached for the bag of chocolate chip cookies she'd purchased at the train station. The bag was surprisingly light. Had she mindlessly eaten the entire contents on the drive?

She rummaged in the bottom of the bag for one last cookie and chewed slowly, vowing to eat healthier tomorrow. The Cherish Hills Inn, the rental she'd booked for the week, boasted a small kitchen, so there were no excuses. Besides, she was a good cook.

Dusting her fingers on a napkin in the glove compartment, she grabbed a bottled water and scooped up her leather briefcase stuffed with music.

Her palms were sweaty. She hesitated.

Fear of what might go wrong stopped her from getting out of the car. It had never occurred to her to let Dr. Gantori know she'd be traveling to another corner of the country. What would happen if she ran out of pain medication or experienced a panic attack and her hands froze to the piano keys?

Get back in the game. Keep God as the priority.

She lowered her car window and gazed outside, focusing on deep breaths in and out.

A fold of sleek silver clouds drifted across a robin's egg blue sky—a typical spring day in South Carolina. She knew the weather by heart. The air was mild, blowing a slight breeze against her cheeks. A hound dog lay basking on the sidewalk in the bright noonday sun.

Relax your muscles. Think positively.

She wiped her palms on her tweed skirt. There were pharmacies everywhere, she assured herself, and Dr. Gantori was merely a phone call away. Still, a knot threatened to take up residence in her stomach. What if the doctor didn't answer when she called?

Her brows puckered, her thoughts scattered. *No, no, no.* She bridled her panic. The task of chastising herself was growing thin as frustration poked through her anxiety. Undoubtedly the doctor used a twenty-four-hour answering service.

She was back in Cherish for her brother, not herself. It was high time she rearranged her priorities. There was more to her story than failing to become a concert performer. Through her difficult year of wrist pain when she'd become angry with God, she'd wanted to run away from her problems, disengaging from friends, social media, and to be truthful, from life.

If only her carpal tunnel hadn't been so excruciating, if only she'd hadn't become addicted to pain relievers ...

If only ... If only ...

But she had, and she'd become an addict.

However, she'd come through the storm intact and had learned to keep her trust in God, because He had her name on something else. But she didn't know what. She only knew it wasn't a concert career.

"Everyone has doubts after a poor performance," Dorothy mumbled, lifting a brief prayer. "What matters is how we react to them."

Holding that thought, she drew her shoulders straight, grabbed her canvas quilted jacket, tasseled purse and briefcase, and stepped from the car.

Her gaze landed on the top step of Memorial Street Church and a rollicking laugh gave her pause.

"Dorothy Thompson, is that really you?" Marge Addyson, the church's associate pastor and the clergy person elected to officiate the wedding ceremony, greeted Dorothy with a flash of a smile that could pass for heat lightning. "Why, you're all grown up. I haven't seen you since your parents went to be with the Lord."

"It's been five years since their funerals." Dorothy gulped air as she replied, that familiar despondency stabbing her heart. Her parent's car accident should never have happened. Her father had always been careful when he drove, mindfully watching the speed limit, and only twenty miles outside of Cherish on the highway near St. Luke's hospital … no one could have predicted a fatal accident where the other driver was strung-out on drugs.

"When did you arrive in Cherish?" Mrs. Addyson asked.

"Just now." Dorothy gazed heavenward, grateful for the change in subject. "I rented a car at the Cherish Central train station." Her proper black pumps echoed across the pavement as she made her way up the church steps. "Where's Pastor Steven and his wife, Christina?"

"They're taking a well-deserved vacation. You're sure to see them both when they return in two weeks."

She wouldn't be staying in Cherish for two weeks, Dorothy thought, although there was no need to share that information with the kind woman.

When Dorothy reached the church's entryway, Mrs. Addyson embraced her in a warm hug. "I'm happy as the bluebonnets blooming in spring that you could come back for Nicholas' wedding. I hope it wasn't difficult taking time away from your prominent concert engagements."

Prominent concert engagements? A distant memory. Paying the rent on her expensive apartment in New York City? Not so distant.

"No worries." Dorothy fingered the corners of her worn leather briefcase. "I'd never refuse my big brother anything, nor miss seeing him and Alice get married."

Nicholas and his fiancée, Alice, had insisted that Dorothy play piano for their wedding. They'd requested contemporary music, although Dorothy had also brought along her favorite classical pieces. What wedding guest wouldn't be stirred to stand when they heard J.S. Bach's "Jesu, Joy of Man's Desiring" for the bride's processional march?

Mrs. Addyson stepped back. "And you're still tall and as pretty as a peppermint parfait. You haven't changed a bit."

"Thank you." Dorothy ran a hand down her brown braid. "You haven't changed either."

Kindness beamed from the elderly woman's crystal blue eyes. "I'm ten years older and infinitely wiser." Her salt and pepper hair had grown a little grayer, had been cut a little shorter.

Dorothy shaded her eyes and peered toward the street. "Did the music store close? When I drove by I noticed the building was vacant and a 'For Sale' sign was on the door."

"Yes, Musically Yours went out of business about a year ago."

Dorothy well remembered racing into Musically Yours on Saturday afternoons, fingering the darkening edges of well-loved classical pieces that emitted a scent of paper and leather-bound volumes of first edition music.

All the memories brought a sense of familiarity. In Cherish, people knew your name. She'd missed those things because she'd found city folks indifferent and uncompromising.

The comfortable warmth of the South Carolina sun hit her face, and her heart felt full for the first time in a long time. She gazed at Memorial Street Church's magnificent steeple with the cross on top, and sadness flickered, disrupting the fullness in her heart. She'd hoped to become so much more than a panic-stricken performer who'd relied on opiates for pain. Despite her brief fame, she'd come back to Cherish with her solitude bigger than ever.

It serves you right, her conscience chattered. *You were a fake in high school, forever seeking approval from your classmates to ensure your popularity. Music became your life, your escape, although you're not great at making music anymore, either.*

"Don't bring your issues to church; bring them directly to God," one of her favorite pastors had once said.

She pushed the steely composure of a seasoned performer into place as Mrs. Addyson hooked an arm around Dorothy's shoulders and led her inside. "I always told your late mother you had an ear for music, honey." She gestured upward to the shiny ebony grand piano in the choir loft. "Is Ryan meeting you here so you two can rehearse?"

Dorothy hesitated. "Ryan who?"

"Ryan Edwards. He and your brother were good friends in high school. He'll be singing the Ave Maria at the wedding ceremony during the offering of the gifts. You're his accompanist."

Dorothy's mouth trembled with surprise.

Ryan Edwards.

She tipped her head back and briefly closed her eyes, visualizing Ryan's skinny build, his quiet demeanor, his booming operatic voice which had prompted his high school classmates to snicker. Often he'd accompanied her to Musically Yours, tendering kind support, encouraging her appreciation of Bach and Beethoven and Mozart. And when he would visit her house, Ryan would bring his precious LP's he'd kept hidden in his room and play Luciano Pavarotti and Placido Domingo recordings for her.

Their friendship had grown, and by the time she reached her early teens, she'd had a mad crush on him. He'd never known because she'd kept a cool demeanor around him. He was the high school nerd, and her popularity was at stake. In hindsight, she was glad she'd never let on how she felt about him because by her high school sophomore year, he was gone.

211

"He's become a well-known opera star in Europe and has flown all the way from Italy at your brother's request. Imagine, two famous musicians in our Lord's house." Mrs. Addyson gave Dorothy's shoulder a slight bump and added a mischievous grin. "When he was younger, that boy got into just enough mischief to make him interesting. Bless his heart, considering his Sunday supper was little more than fried water, his family was so poor. We're mighty proud of all he's accomplished. He's a few years older than you, so you may not remember him."

"He was my best friend," Dorothy murmured. She set her music briefcase on a back pew and rubbed her forehead. "Nicholas mentioned nothing about Ryan singing."

"These days, your brother is busy between getting ready to graduate from the police academy and the wedding plans. It must've slipped his mind." Mrs. Addyson peered up and read the clock in the choir loft. "Ryan was supposed to be here at one o'clock and he's obviously running late, unless he's canceled altogether and sent a replacement singer. I won't detain you any longer."

"Thanks. I'll get started then."

"Don't forget dinner at The Garden Terrace tonight for the pre-wedding celebration." Mrs. Addyson winked and patted Dorothy's arm. "Your brother said he's treating everyone."

"I wouldn't miss *that* first for the world."

Now if she could only get herself to sit down at the piano and play something.

She willed her heart to stop pounding, willed her pulse to stop racing.

Grimacing, she managed a smile. "See you tonight, Mrs. Addyson."

You have nothing to prove to anyone but God, and he's not judging. The thought came quick through Dorothy's mind.

Taking a long swallow, she made her way up the stairs to the choir loft.

*** End of Excerpt *A Love Song To Cherish* by Josie Riviera ***

Copyright © 2018 Josie Riviera

Keep reading on Amazon. FREE on Kindle Unlimited.

ABOUT THE AUTHOR

Josie Riviera is a *USA TODAY* bestselling author of contemporary, inspirational, and historical sweet romances that read like Hallmark movies. She lives in the Charlotte, NC, area with her wonderfully supportive husband. They share their home with an adorable shih tzu, who constantly needs grooming, and live in an old house forever needing renovations.

To receive my Newsletter and your free sweet romance novella ebook as a thank you gift, sign up HERE.

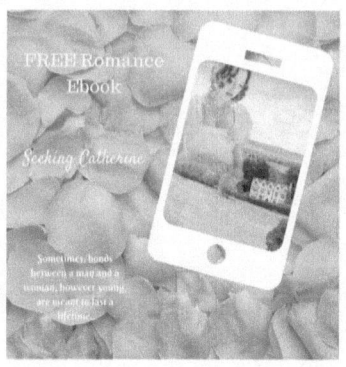

Become a member of my Read and Review VIP Facebook group for exclusive giveaways and ARCs.

josieriviera.com/

ACKNOWLEDGMENTS

An appreciative thank you to my patient husband, Dave, and our three wonderful children.

ALSO BY JOSIE RIVIERA

Seeking Patience

Seeking Catherine (always Free!)

Seeking Fortune

Seeking Charity

Seeking Rachel

The Seeking Series

Oh Danny Boy

I Love You More

A Snowy White Christmas

A Portuguese Christmas

Holiday Hearts Book Bundle Volume One

Holiday Hearts Book Bundle Volume Two

Holiday Hearts Book Bundle Volume Three

Holiday Hearts Book Bundle Volume Four

Holiday Hearts Book Bundle Volume Five

Candleglow and Mistletoe

Maeve (Perfect Match)

A Christmas To Cherish

A Love Song To Cherish

A Valentine To Cherish

A Christmas Puppy To Cherish

A Homecoming To Cherish

Romance Stories To Cherish

Aloha to Love

Sweet Peppermint Kisses

Valentine Hearts Boxed Set

1-800-CUPID

1-800-CHRISTMAS

1-800-IRELAND

1-800-SUMMER

1-800-NEW YEAR

Irish Hearts Sweet Romance Bundle

Holly's Gift

A Chocolate-Box Valentine

A Chocolate-Box Christmas

A Chocolate-Box New Years

A Chocolate-Box Summer Breeze

A Chocolate-Box Christmas Wish

A Chocolate-Box Irish Wedding

Chocolate-Box Hearts

Chocolate-Box Hearts Volume Two

Chocolate-Box Double Hearts

Recipes from the Heart

Leading Hearts

New Year Hearts

SENIOR HEARTS

A Summer To Cherish

Summer Hearts

Romance Stories To Cherish Volume Two

Cherished Hearts

Christmas in the Air

A Very Christian Christmas

The 1-800-Series Volume Two

The 1-800-Series Complete

Christmas Tails of the Heart

Cocoa's Christmas Love

Pawfect Christmas Hearts

Pink Coral Island

Most books are available in ebook, audiobook, paperback, Large Print paperback and Hardcover.

Many are FREE on Kindle Unlimited!